by Anne Mather
comes to life
on the movie screen

starring
KEIR DULLEA · SUSAN PENHALIGON

Leopard *in the* Snow

Guest Stars
KENNETH MORE · BILLIE WHITELAW

featuring GORDON THOMSON as MICHAEL
and JEREMY KEMP as BOLT

Produced by JOHN QUESTED and CHRIS HARROP
Screenplay by ANNE MATHER and JILL HYEM
Directed by GERRY O'HARA
An Anglo-Canadian Co-Production

Dream of Winter

by

REBECCA STRATTON

Harlequin Books

TORONTO • LONDON • NEW YORK • AMSTERDAM • SYDNEY

Original hardcover edition published in 1977
by Mills & Boon Limited

ISBN 0-373-02154-2

Harlequin edition published April 1978

PRINTED IN U.S.A.

CHAPTER ONE

THERE had been more snow during the night and Brunnenheim sparkled like a fairytale village under the dazzling whiteness of it. The peak of the Schillenberg looked almost close enough to touch as it soared up into the clear blue sky and the thick snow on its upper reaches was dyed gold by the morning sun. It was a sight that always inspired Sophie whenever she looked from her window and saw it, and it was even more breathtaking at sunset when the evening light stained the whole magnificent peak a deep rosy crimson.

Switzerland was a country that presented such breathtaking scenes as a matter of course, and Sophie could even forget the occasional discomfort of her present situation for most of the time and enjoy herself. She loved the clear light air, and the mountains that swept down into valleys, cradling little villages like Brunnenheim in their midst, or balancing them precariously part way down a tree-clad slope.

Even this early in the day the occasional figure could be seen on the distant slopes, speeding silently downward over the immaculate whiteness of last night's new fall and weaving around the dark fingers of pine that thrust through the snow at an angle, with drifts piled against their resistant trunks.

Sophie always envied the skiers, especially the really

skilled people, for they came closest to really conquering those incredibly beautiful and deceptively tranquil peaks. Once, she had promised herself that she would come skimming down from the dizzying height of Mädchen Turm and into the village without pausing; but that had been what now seemed like a lifetime ago.

She half turned as she stood in the window of her room, thinking she heard a sound from the next room. Claude was still sleeping and Flora, his mother, would not put in an appearance for at least another hour. It might be possible to slip out for a few minutes and enjoy the crisp newness of the morning alone, with no one the wiser, but she hesitated to go in case Claude woke and she was not within call. Also, she noted, Karl was already up and about, and that was deterrent enough in itself.

Sophie drew back slightly from the shuttered window as the tall figure of a man emerged from the entrance of the hotel almost immediately below her window. She did not want to meet up with Karl so early in the day. For one thing because if Flora heard of it she would immediately suspect an ulterior motive, and for another because Sophie always felt much too uncomfortable in Karl's presence now.

There was a time, three years ago, when she had felt very differently about Karl Bruner, but then she had been only eighteen years old and dazzled by the charm and reputation of a man of the world who was also a champion skier. Even though he was quite a bit older than she was, and had never given her cause to think he saw her as anything other than a charming and rather naïve young girl on holiday with her father, she had dreamed that one day he would ask her to marry him. At that time anything had seemed possible.

Not that it was Karl Bruner who shattered her dreams; her own change of circumstances had achieved that. Three years ago Sophie had been able to enjoy herself without a care in the world. Her father had indulged her every whim and denied her nothing. Until one day when he was killed in an air crash and the dream had suddenly become a nightmare.

The bitter truth had been brought home to her that there was virtually nothing left of the wealth she had for so long taken for granted. The life of ease had come to an abrupt end and she had been forced to face life not only without her father, but without the kind of life he had brought her up to expect.

Sophie was untrained for anything that equipped her for earning her own living, and she had been almost overwhelmingly grateful when a second cousin on her mother's side had offered her the job of caring for her little son. Flora Dauzan was recently divorced from her French millionaire husband, and she saw in Sophie's impoverished helplessness an opportunity to acquire the services of a willing nursemaid without the expense involved in paying a professional.

Flora Dauzan begrudged paying out money for any other reason than for her own pleasure or comfort. The jet-setting wife of a millionaire had begun life as Florence Adams, the daughter of Sophie's mother's cousin. A brief but successful career as a model had led to marriage and, almost as quickly, to divorce, but Flora had acquired a taste of high living that she would not easily forgo—she had said so quite frankly to Sophie.

Claude, her son, went everywhere with her. Not because Flora could not bear to be parted from him, but because to date he was his father's only child, and heir to the Dauzan millions; a prospect she had no intention of relinquishing. Sometimes Sophie almost hated her for her attitude towards the little boy, although Claude seemed happy enough in his own way.

With her mind on other matters Sophie did not realise at first that she had been spotted, despite her efforts to stay out of sight. Down in the street, standing amid his own dark tracks in the new snow, Karl Bruner looked up at her window and waved a hand, a greeting she could do little else but acknowledge.

He was tall and lean and, Sophie now readily admitted, almost insufferably arrogant, but he was still undeniably attractive to her, as he was to most women. At eighteen she had found his mature charm quite devastating, and even now, three years later, she could understand her own youthful infatuation with him. Only now she saw him as not only unattainable, but less heroically perfect. He was a man and not the demigod she had seen him as three years before.

Close-fitting ski-trousers emphasised the length of his legs and ski-boots added to his height, while the thickness of a sweater and windcheater jacket added bulk to a broad chest and shoulders above lean hips. His head was bare because the hood of the jacket was pushed back and he carried the wool cap he would wear on the slopes, tucked into a pocket. Thick golden hair flopped across his forehead the way it always did, and his brown face creased in a smile that was reflected in bright blue eyes.

Sophie always felt very self-conscious when Karl looked at her, even now, when she was fully recovered from her earlier hero-worship. Karl Bruner liked good-looking women and it would have been false modesty not to recognise her own physical attractions. From her father she had inherited her thick dark hair, and from her mother her hazel eyes that slanted so intriguingly at their corners, and a soft full mouth that always looked slightly vulnerable. Her face and figure belonged to the category known as petite, but her shape was feminine enough not to be overlooked by anyone as knowledge-able on the subject as Karl.

'Good morning, Sophie!' His English was slightly pedantic, but scarcely accented, and he waved a gloved hand in greeting. 'Are you coming to join me?'

He must know she couldn't go, Sophie thought, and for a moment resented his thoughtlessness. When she had known him in the old days she had lived in hope of his one day issuing such an invitation, but he never had, and she wondered if he did so now only because he knew she could not leave Claude.

She shook her head rather than make a verbal reply, because if she woke Claude in the adjoining room he would want her attention, and she wanted a few more minutes to herself before another day began. Also if Flora happened to be awake and heard them exchang-ing greetings she would be angry. Karl Bruner, Flora had left no one in any doubt, was going to be her second husband. He was just as wealthy as Rudi Dauzan, her ex-husband, and far more attractive.

Only one thing stood in the way of the plan becom-ing fact, and that was Karl himself. He was an attentive companion to any woman he happened to be with, but nothing in his manner suggested that he viewed Flora with any particular favour. It was a fact that could, on occasion, bring Flora to the point of hurling the articles on her dressing-table all over the room in angry frustra-tion.

'Sophie?'

He still stood down there looking up at her, and Sophie wished he would simply go away. He was obviously heading for the slopes to get in some practice before too many people were about, so she could not have joined him anyway.

'I can't, Karl.'

She used his christian name only when Flora was not about; at other times he was very formally Mr Bruner, although she did it only to avoid trouble with Flora. Karl noticed it, however, and she was sure it amused him.

'No?' He smiled once more and shrugged his broad shoulders. 'O.K., I will see you later, hmm?'

That fascinating suggestion of an accent could still bring a flutter of reaction from her, she realised with a sigh. Sounding the 'w' as a 'v'; only a bare suggestion of it, but enough to sound intriguingly different. She watched him go, making for the cable-car at the far end of the village, and for once allowed herself to brood on the past.

At eighteen she would have given her right arm to go with him, and found some way of accepting that casual invitation, but at twenty-one she knew it was out of the question and accepted the fact. Also she was far less starry-eyed about Karl Bruner. As soon as she saw him disappear behind the *Gasthaus* on the corner of the street, she turned back into her room; it was time she got Claude up.

The boy was already awake, sitting up in bed and smiling when she went into his room. An attractive child, he had his mother's good looks combined with his father's colouring. With finely chiselled features, even in babyhood, and a small face, he had dark hair and brown eyes that could look infinitely appealing, and quite often did. He spoke excellent English, for he was bi-lingual even at four years old, and Sophie was very fond of him.

'Good morning, Claude. Are you ready for your bath?'

'Are we going on the cable-car today, Sophie?' He invariably answered a question with another, but he was already out of bed and making for the bathroom, so clearly he was anxious to be up and about. 'We could go to the top, and see the Weitlauf from the Mädchen Turm, yes?'

How on earth he managed to get his tongue round the German names, Sophie could not understand, for she still had trouble with them. 'We'll see,' she told him, helping him off with his pyjamas. 'For the moment we'll concentrate on having a bath and then breakfast.'

He was amenable, very much so, and Sophie loved his charmingly old-fashioned manners—something he owed, she knew, more to the influence of his Grandmother Dauzan than to Flora, who had little time for him. Washed and dressed he looked very sweet and handsome, and Sophie took a delight in taking him into the restaurant with her.

Maybe some of the other guests thought he was her son; if they did she was not averse to the error, and he certainly showed more affection towards her than he did towards his mother. Sophie had a way with children, Flora did not.

He held Sophie's hand while they returned to their rooms after breakfast, and it was only while she was putting on his outdoor things that he questioned her again about where they were going. 'May we go up to the Mädchen Turm, Sophie, please?'

Glancing out of the window, Sophie gave it some thought. Karl was out there somewhere and if they used the cable-car and went as high as the Maiden's Tower there was a distinct possibility that they would bump into him. Claude would not mind, he liked Karl, but he would in all probability mention it to his mother, and that would cause suspicion.

It was very difficult to resist that appealing look of Claude's, however, and he was quite set on going to the highest point on the cable. After a moment or two, she shrugged and smiled, yielding to the inevitable. 'Very well,' she conceded, 'but only if your *maman* says we may.'

Claude shrugged. It was amazing how eloquently French he could seem when he did that, even at four years old, and his dark eyes were gravely confident. 'I will ask her, Sophie; but she will not mind.'

It was unlikely that Flora would mind where they went, Sophie knew, as long as she was not troubled with the proximity of her son when she had other things to do, but it was rather early to expect her to be wakeful enough to answer questions.

'I don't think your *maman* will be up yet,' Sophie warned him, but Claude was already knocking on his mother's bedroom door.

The shrill sharpness of the voice that told him to come in suggested that Flora was not feeling her best yet, and inevitably it would be Sophie who bore the brunt of her annoyance. Perhaps it would have been better to follow her charge through to his mother's room, but she stayed where she was and tidied his things, listening through the open doors to their conversation.

She heard Claude ask permission to go up to the

Maiden's Tower, and she heard Flora's impatient agreement, followed by a curt dismissal. 'For heaven's sake go away, it's too early to come bothering me with questions! Isn't Sophie up yet?'

'Yes, I'm up, Flora.' She walked along to the next room and stood in the doorway, looking at Flora propped up in bed and looking grumpily half-asleep. 'Good morning. I thought it best to get your permission before I took Claude on the cable-car. I'm sorry if he disturbed you.'

Flora Dauzan was handsome rather than pretty. Her features were small and clean-cut and she had quite nice eyes, except that they so often looked sharp with annoyance, as now. Her hair was naturally light brown, but she had long since disguised its mediocrity with a bright gold that she felt was more in keeping with the image of an internationally famous model, and she had the almost shapeless figure that was necessary for her original profession.

Normally she never allowed anyone to see her until she was perfectly dressed and immaculately made up, but at the moment her face had a curiously naked look, so characteristic of someone who habitually wore a great deal of make-up, and her rather small mouth was pursed in annoyance as she glared at Sophie from her bed.

'Fancy letting him disturb me at this ghastly hour,' she complained in her slightly harsh voice. 'I don't care where you go with him, it's your responsibility where he goes and what he does as long as he doesn't come to any harm! What do you imagine I pay you for?'

In fact she paid very little for the services she expected, but Sophie was too thankful to have the job of looking after Claude to raise that question. She took

Claude's hand in hers and nodded. 'I'm sorry, Flora.'
Closing the door carefully behind them, she looked
down at the little boy with a rueful smile. 'Shall we
go?' she asked. It was always so difficult not to feel sorry
for him, and yet by now Claude scarcely noticed his
mother's lack of affection, she thought.

'To the Mädchen Turm?' he asked, and she nodded.
'If that's where you'd like to go.'

The boy looked up at her, his small face flushed
with anticipation and his eyes bright and sparkling. 'I
heard Karl,' he told her. 'Perhaps he is skiing, yes?'

'I expect so.'

She did not commit herself to any more, but she was
aware of Claude's brief scrutiny before the excitement
of their outing overcame everything else. Sometimes,
she thought, Claude's manner was much too old for a
four-year-old, and he noticed too much. It would never
do for him to harbour ideas about her and Karl, or it
would make things impossible for her with Flora.

There was something strangely exhilarating about being suspended above the sweeping panorama of snow
and dark pines, gliding smoothly upward on the slender
cables hung between towering pylons. It was an experience that Sophie always enjoyed anew each time she
travelled up from the valley to the highest point on the
cable-car route.

Usually the cars were filled with skiers on their way
to the various skiing slopes, but it was fairly early yet
and there had been the usual round of après-ski gather-
ings last night; most of the crowd would come a little
later. At the moment there were no more than three or
four people sharing their airborne car.

Down below the village slid away, becoming more

and more toylike as distance diminished its size, and the long sweeping ski runs were fresh and deep after last night's fall, slashed across by ragged lines of dark pine acting as a safety barrier against avalanches. The real enthusiasts were already making tracks in the new snow, and a briefly seen figure in a bright blue jacket could have been Karl Bruner, weaving his way downward with the skill and breathtaking grace that never failed to impress her.

Not that it was possible to positively identify anyone at this distance, but Karl had been wearing a bright blue ski jacket when she spoke to him earlier, and he invariably wore the same red wool cap on his fair head. Blue jackets and red caps, however, were in common use on the slopes and except to the experts on style one skier looked much like another at speed.

It was warm in the cable-car and Claude had his jacket unfastened at the neck, showing the thick white sweater he wore underneath a red jacket and trousers. Kneeling on the seat beside Sophie, he pressed his nose to the glass, trying to follow the progress of the flying figure as far as he could, his eyes bright and envious.

Claude wanted to be able to ski more than anything, but Flora would never hear of it—he was far too precious to risk his life. He was not even allowed on to the nursery slopes with the other little ones, who daily slid happily on their miniature skis down gentle slopes, under the expert guidance of patient instructors.

'There's been more snow in the night.' She turned her head and spoke close to his ear, smiling at his expression of utter concentration. 'Isn't it lovely and white down there?'

Claude was much too engrossed to reply, but he nodded and raised himself an inch or two higher, so that he could see a fraction more of the mountain side, and the skier. It was then that Sophie became conscious of the man seated opposite to them, for he was looking at Claude with an understanding smile, as if he knew exactly how he felt.

He was brown-haired and thin-faced, not a very noticeable man in the normal course of things, but he had a pleasant smile when he caught her eye, and his accent when he spoke suggested that he was as English as she was herself.

'An enthusiast?' He inclined his head towards Claude and smiled.

'A fanatic!' Sophie agreed, a protective arm across Claude's back in case he should turn suddenly and topple off his seat. 'I don't think I ever saw a four-year-old so completely absorbed.'

'It's nice to find it in a little chap like that.' He noted the fact that she was not wearing ski-boots, and a long jacket instead of the necessary windcheater. 'You're not skiing?'

'I started to learn years ago, I got—moderately proficient, but——' She shrugged, uneasily reminded of those days with her father, when she had spent so much time on the ski slopes and so little time learning, because she had watched Karl practise instead—standing in the concealment of the clustered pines, hoping to remain unseen while he skimmed past her time and again, never satisfied with his own excellence. 'I often wish now that I'd gone on with it.'

'It's a pity you didn't, there's so much to enjoy.'

Recognising another enthusiast, Sophie smiled. 'You're obviously as much an enthusiast as Claude is!'

'It's the most exhilarating experience in the world!' His fervour attracted Claude's attention and the child turned and gazed at him with frank curiosity.

'I wish I could learn.' He spoke up with uncharacter-
istic boldness and his dark eyes sparkled eagerly. 'I
want to be the most famous skier in the world one day!'

'Why not?' The man treated his dream seriously, and
not at all as if he found such childish daydreaming
amusing. 'But you must start learning now, while
you're still very young. It's the best thing.' He spoke as
much to Sophie, she realised, as to Claude, so that she
suspected he had come to the inevitable conclusion.
'Have you asked your mother if you can learn?'

'Oh yes.' Claude was quite unaware of any misconception, and he looked incredibly soulful about being
deprived of his dearest ambition. 'Maman says I cannot
learn.'

The stranger had grey eyes, rather nice friendly eyes,
and they regarded her seriously. 'You should let him,
you know. It isn't a bit dangerous if he's properly
taught. Quite tiny tots learn to ski.'

Sophie was too accustomed to the mistake to feel any
embarrassment herself, but she tried to correct the
wrong impression without making it sound too important. 'It isn't up to me, I'm afraid; I'm Claude's
nursemaid, not his mother.'

'Oh, I see. I'm sorry.' A faint flush coloured his rather
pale face, and Sophie sought hastily to make up for his
discomfiture.

'Oh, I'm quite used to being taken for his mother, I
really don't mind,' she told him. 'And neither does
Claude, do you?'

Claude simply nodded instead of confirming it ver-
bally, for it was doubtful if he fully appreciated the
meaning of what they said. His eyes were on the snow
slopes again and he pressed his nose to the glass, trying

to get a better view of a figure that came schussing downwards from the dizzying height of the Mädchen Turm. No more than a streak of blue and red amid the flurry of fresh snow that spumed up from his skis as he made a turn.

'There's Karl!' He pointed a stubby forefinger and his voice was crackling with excitement, though it was doubtful if he really could identify the skier. 'It *is* Karl, Sophie, see how fast he goes! I *wish* I could do that!'

'A friend of yours?'

The smile was friendly and encouraging and Claude nodded. He was a sociable child, always ready to make new friends, and especially if they shared his enthusiasm for skiing. 'Karl Bruner is very famous,' he informed him solemnly. 'He is the best skier in all the world.'

'Karl Bruner?' The man looked interested. 'I heard he was staying here. Do you know him?'

He asked the question of Sophie, and she found it difficult to answer him as freely as she might have done without Claude beside her. But she nodded and half-smiled, admitting it without being too enthusiastic and giving the wrong impression.

'Slightly,' she said. 'He's staying at the same hotel as we are in the village.'

'Hotel Schillenberg?' He appeared delighted with the information. 'I'm there too, though I only arrived early this morning.'

'It *must* have been early,' Sophie smiled. 'I thought we were early birds, but if you've only just arrived——'

'I had a bite of breakfast, then couldn't resist coming up to look at the view. It's my favourite view, and I've seen some pretty wonderful ones at different times.'

He extended a hand towards her. 'My name's St John—Robert St John.'

Sophie felt almost ashamed of herself for not recognising her own country's representative, but most newspaper photographs showed Bobby St John wearing a mask-like helmet and goggles as he sped downhill, a blurred figure amid plumes of snow thrown up by his skis. His face was quite unknown to her, but nevertheless she felt she should apologise for her ignorance.

'I should have recognised you, Mr St John; my name's Sophie Roberts—how do you do?'

'And you're English?'

She nodded and turned to introduce Claude, who was already attracted by the familiar name. There was scarcely a name in skiing that he did not know. 'This is Claude Dauzan—Claude, you know of Mr St John, don't you?'

'Yes.'

He offered his hand solemnly, and yet again Sophie was touched by his charming good manners. He was obviously intrigued with the idea of meeting another of the big names in person, and he sat round straight in his seat, taking an interest now that something close at hand provided a distraction.

'Dauzan?' The recognition of names was mutual, and Robert St John was probably as aware of the Dauzan family situation as the rest of the world was, thanks to world-wide press coverage of his parents' divorce. 'And you're French, right?'

Claude nodded. 'Only half French,' he corrected firmly but politely. 'Maman is English—she is Sophie's——'

He looked to Sophie for guidance, their tangled

family connections confused him, and she smiled, feeling suddenly uneasy about explaining her relationship to Flora, though she never had before. 'Mrs Dauzan is my second cousin,' she told Robert St John. 'It's not a very close tie really.'

'Maman and Sophie are friends with Karl too,' Claude informed him, obviously intent on making everything quite clear. 'But Sophie does not like him much.'

'Claude!' She felt herself blushing, and hastily bent to adjust the set of Claude's jacket collar; anything to hide her face for a second or two while she recovered her composure. His childish frankness could be very embarrassing sometimes, and yet she could hardly blame him for it. 'We're almost there now, I think you'd better have your hat on and put up your hood.'

'Oh no, not yet, Sophie.' Claude watched the people alighting at the intermediate station, and made no attempt to adjust his hood. He knew the route to the Mädchen Turm by heart, and there was some distance to go to the top yet. 'We shan't see Karl, because he has already gone.'

'Never mind, you'll see him when we get down again, I expect.'

It was almost inevitable that they would see Karl, she thought, for he was frequently in the same crowd that Flora moved in and, while she and Claude never actually joined them, they were sometimes to be found somewhere on the edge of the party, trying to remain unobtrusive. In the evenings, when Claude had been put to bed, things were sometimes difficult for Sophie, for she was not expected to show herself in too close proximity to Flora, and she had little liking for lone expeditions.

She was aware that Robert St John was still taking an interest and she wondered if he too was likely to become one of Flora's crowd of friends at the hotel. He was a well-known name, and Flora was adept at acquiring new and interesting men as they arrived. She had only now noticed that he did not have skis with him, and she smiled enquiringly at him.

'You're not skiing?' she asked, then suddenly remembered that he had been injured quite seriously during practice several weeks ago. 'Oh no, of course, you've been laid up, haven't you? I read about it in the papers.'

'I'm hoping to get back into action again during the next few weeks. It's rotten getting myself hurt just when everything's happening.'

'And we *need* you!'

He laughed, a slight flush betraying modesty such as Karl would never have admitted to. 'I suppose so,' he allowed. 'Although there are one or two really good youngsters coming along now; I have to look to my laurels!' He glanced down at the slope below them and his face was thoughtful. 'Not only the youngsters either; Karl Bruner is still far too good for my comfort, even though he is well into his thirties. He's a fantastic skier.'

'He's the best in the whole world,' Claude insisted, determined to have full credit for his hero, and Robert St John smiled ruefully.

'You could well be right by next month this time,' he allowed.

'We're here!' Claude's excited voice cut short Sophie's attempt to reply, and she hastily drew him towards her, pulling on the red woollen hat he had chosen because it was like the one Karl wore. 'Can we have coffee in the restaurant, Sophie? Can we, please?'

'Yes, if you'd like to.' She smiled at Robert St John, half apologetically, because the child must necessarily make normal adult conversation difficult, but he too was smiling and looking at Claude with genuine liking. 'We can watch the slopes from the window over there; shall we sit there?'

'May I be allowed to join you?' Sophie had been half expecting the request, in fact she had been ready to invite him if he had been too reticent to ask, and she smiled unhesitatingly.

'Yes, of course, please do.'

'Then in exchange for your company please let me get the coffee; may I?'

'Thank you.'

She asked that Claude's should be very white, for he had only lately developed a passion for coffee and she was not at all sure that too much, too strong was good for him. Her own she chose to have black and yielded to the suggestion of cognac to counter the clean coldness of the alpine air. There was no waitress service, only a glass-topped counter behind which a smiling Swiss-Italian girl dispensed a staggering variety of beverages and pastries.

There were few other people about as yet, and the glass-walled building had rather a spartan air about it. Plain wood walls below the glass, and a floor serviceable enough to cope with the many thousands of booted feet that scuffed over its surface during the winter season. It was lit by strip lighting, but there was a curious kind of luminous look too that stemmed from the vastness of the snow slopes. It was warm without being in the least cosy.

Claude was interested in nothing but what was going

on on the slopes and he watched another flying figure launch itself from below the jutting, tower-like rock that was known as the Maiden's Tower—a rock from which, so fable had it, a young girl had once thrown herself to her death rather than marry a man she did not love. It was directly opposite where they sat, a vast, glowering outcrop, iced on top with fresh snow, like the turret of a castle.

'Fast, so fast!' Claude's excited voice shrilled out, his nose pressed to the glass window as he peered downwards, following the skier's progress down the winding, dazzling white run. 'Oh, Sophie, see how fast he goes!'

'Yes, it's wonderful!' She shared his enthusiasm, though not quite so wholeheartedly, and she too was smiling as she watched the flying figure that could just as easily have been female, though she did not bother to point that out. 'It's rather like flying, isn't it, Claude?'

'It is exactly like flying!' Both heads turned swiftly at the sound of a familiar voice, and Sophie's breath caught in her throat when she found herself looking up into Karl Bruner's tanned and smiling face. 'I did not know that you intended to come up here, Sophie; you did not say so when I spoke to you earlier.'

Caught unawares and feeling discomfitingly awkward, Sophie glanced almost involuntarily across to where Robert St John was making his way back with their coffee. 'I didn't know then.' She laughed and looked at Claude, now more interested in the newcomer than in the lone skier outside. 'Claude decided we were coming.'

'And now that you are here, I may buy you coffee, yes?'

He was smiling; confident as ever, and for some reason Sophie hated having to tell him that their coffee was already on its way. 'That's very kind of you, Karl, but we already have some coming.' She indicated the man coming up behind him. 'We met Mr St John in the cable-car and he offered to buy us coffee.'

For a second only, a fleeting frown crossed Karl's ruggedly sensual features, then he was smiling again, turning to speak to Robert St John as he came to join them, looking vaguely uneasy. 'Ah!' As soon as the tray was safely deposited on the table, Karl extended a large brown hand and his blue eyes gleamed in friendly curiosity. 'It is Bobby St John, is it not? Karl Bruner—we have never actually met, I think.'

'I'm glad to meet you.' They shook hands and it all seemed very friendly, but then there was a short and very meaningful silence before their host spoke again. 'Er—can I get you coffee too?' he offered.

'Oh no, thank you.' Karl's expressive hands denied any need for such service. 'I was about to leave when I saw two old friends sitting here.'

He made the claim casually and yet left no doubt that he was in some way trying to impress the other man with his prior interest, and Sophie saw the curiosity in Robert St John's eyes, even though he was too polite to let it show in any other way.

'If you care to join us, do so by all means,' he urged, but Karl was shaking his head.

'I would not dream of interrupting you,' he told him with pedantic politeness. 'I shall take my second run now, I think, if you will excuse me.' He smiled down at Claude as he pulled on the red wool hat that the boy admired so much. 'You will watch me from the window, eh, Claude?'

'Oh, yes!'

Hero-worship gleamed in Claude's dark eyes, and he

watched the tall figure disappear outside; watched while he adjusted goggles and skis to his liking, then gasped in admiration when the tall lean figure sped down the mountainside, throwing up a spume of white in his wake. He kept his eyes on him until he was out of sight, right down below the barrier of spiky pines that thrust into his line of vision. Then he turned and sighed deeply in satisfaction.

'I *will* be glad when Karl is my father,' he said wistfully, and Sophie felt herself flush bright pink when Robert St John looked across at her in obvious surprise.

The idea must have originated with his mother, and Sophie did not see how she could contradict it outright; apart from which she was in no position to know whether or not there was any fact among the wishful thinking of both Claude and his mother.

'Claude——' She stopped herself, for she did not know how to warn a child of four about starting gossip. And next to learning to ski, acquiring Karl as a stepfather was probably what Claude wanted most in the world. 'Drink your coffee,' she said.

CHAPTER TWO

IT was not completely unexpected when Robert St John was almost immediately drawn into Flora's orbit, for he was no less flattered by her obvious interest in him than any other man would have been. Nevertheless Sophie found his willing response to her cousin rather disappointing, for she had looked for more level-headedness from him. Flora, of course, could be very charming when she chose to be, and he was sufficiently well known for her to put herself out for him.

Ever since his arrival at the hotel a couple of days ago, he had spent most of his time with Flora and her group, although to do him justice, Sophie thought he looked rather put out when he realised that she was not invited too. He had joined her and Claude for coffee the morning following his arrival, but then Flora had come along and whisked him away, so pressingly inviting that it would mave been difficult for him to refuse. For a moment it had looked as if he might suggest Sophie and Claude went too, but Flora had almost completely ignored them both and eventually he had said nothing, though it was plain he was uneasy about leaving them.

As usual when Claude had been put to bed, Sophie was faced with a more or less solitary evening. Flora was definitely against her joining her and her friends, and Sophie usually found some quiet little café and sat and watched the crowds. Sooner or later someone usually came along who was ready to chat for a while, but it was still rather lonely for her.

The village had its own kind of beauty at this time of the day. With the lights from houses, cafés and hotels shining out on to snowy streets, it had a fairytale air that was enchanting, and Sophie loved it. She could stroll along and look into the windows of the shops, and listen to the sound of music and laughter, only somehow it would have been so much more enjoyable if there had been someone to share it with. Not for a moment would she have admitted to the same feelings she had known three years ago, but it was a fact that someone like Karl would have made a great deal of difference to her enjoyment.

Not for the first time since she started working for Flora six months ago it crossed her mind that her second cousin was something of a martinet. She discouraged friendships of any sort because, she insisted, they would interfere with the job of caring for Claude. It had only lately occurred to Sophie that Flora was wary of losing a very convenient and low-paid employee to someone else, but she had hastily dismissed the thought. She needed Flora as much as Flora needed her.

The main street of Brunnenheim lay before her like a white ribbon patterned with yellow dots of light, and she walked the whole length of it until she came to the small square from which the cable-cars started their climb to the peak of Schillenberg.

The terminus had been built on to the end of the village; it was part of it, in fact, and in daylight the square was invariably filled with people entering and leaving the cars. Only at this time of the day was it quiet and the lighted buildings deserted except for a

few venturesome spirits taking a slow ride to the top
to look at the breathtaking sight of the slopes by moonlight.

Beyond the yellow lights of the village the mountain
rose, silver-white in the moonlight, up into the clear
blue-black sky, and a cable-car swung slowly, moving
upward like a tiny glowworm against its glistening
slopes. The snowy massif was a vast and awe-inspiring
sight, and it never failed to touch some response in her,
especially at night.

The air was crisp and cold and promised more snow
by morning, so that she pulled the collar of her jacket
up around her ears as she watched the ascending cable-
car. There seemed to be a party going on in a restaurant
just across the square, and the sounds of a pop music
group sounded somehow jarringly alien in this setting,
so that she walked on a little way, trying to get out of
earshot.

The attendant in the ticket office glanced up, only
vaguely curious, as she passed, to stand at the far
corner of the building where she would be less overwhelmed by the sounds of revelry, though still able to
hear them. When she had stayed there with her father
three years before, she had joined in parties like that
and seen nothing amiss with the idea of pop music
amid the peace and quiet of the Alps. Perhaps, she
thought a little ruefully, it was being on her own that
made her dislike it so much now.

The thick sweater she wore was hooded and the hood
drawn up to cover her dark hair, but her cheeks tingled
with the cold air that turned every breath into a cloud
of vapour, and gave her a startlingly wide-awake feeling
that banished every trace of the lethargy she had felt in

the artificial warmth of her hotel bedroom. Leaning against the corner of the terminal building, she gazed up at the mountains and once again experienced that sense of exhilaration they could inspire in her.

Then from across the square she realised that the sounds of the party had become suddenly louder, and she turned her head to see the reason. People came pouring from the restaurant in a confusion of colour and sound, their voices raised, laughing at nothing in particular but simply bent on enjoying themselves, and the little square seemed to fill to overflowing.

They milled around for a few minutes, apparently aimlessly, then turned as if by some common compulsion in the direction of the cable station and surged en masse towards the building where Sophie stood in the shadows. Startled for a moment, she straightened up, watching their approach curiously.

One tall slim figure led the way, the rest simply following. Waving her arms and shouting encouragement to her followers, she came on across the square and, recognising her, Sophie wondered what venture Flora was bent on now. Flora could be almost childish in her excitement and seemed to have the ability to inject others with the same enthusiasm, but she was likely to be less than pleased if she knew her antics were being watched by Sophie. It was a strange fact, but Sophie sometimes felt that having her around could make Flora feel uneasy, though heaven knew why.

Her bright golden head was bare, the hood she wore thrown back, and her hair gleamed in the lights as she called to her companions to follow her, never doubting that they would. Her thin, almost boyishly lean figure was clad in a scarlet ski-suit embroidered with white and gold, and she wore black sealskin boots and mitts. She was not pretty, but Flora was never less than striking, and she was fully aware of it.

As far as she could tell, no one noticed Sophie standing at the corner of the squat wood and glass buildings, for they were all much too caught up in their wild enthusiasm for whatever it was they had in mind. Excitedly talking and laughing, all at one time it seemed, they streamed across the square and into the terminal, following the lead that Flora set, and not really caring where it led them. Somewhere among them, it was almost certain, was Robert St John, and probably Karl too, he sometimes was. Following Flora, wherever she led them.

Hoping to remain uninvolved, Sophie stayed where she was, in the shadows at the end of the ticket office, with the collar of her dark jacket pulled up round her face and the concealing hood of her thick sweater helping to disguise her. She did not want Flora to see her and question her being there, and there was no chance of slipping past unseen now.

From the chatter that was going on when the party reached the office, she gathered that the intention was to take the cable-car up to the restaurant near the Mädchen Turm and carry on their party there. The man in the pay-booth was a little overwhelmed, but he coped well enough, his pedantic German-Swiss accented English dealing politely with the demand for tickets and information about how long they had before the cars stopped running.

It took some time for them all to be accommodated in the overcrowded cars, and the ones that went on first were shouting to the ones left behind, so that it was pandemonium for a while, and Sophie waited for the last of them to be gone so that quiet could return.

It was while she stood waiting for the last crowd, jostling and laughing their way into another car, that an arm suddenly fastened itself around her waist and drew her out of the concealing shadows. It was a masculine arm, steel-hard and refusing to allow her to struggle free of it, hauling her along into the crowd as she tried to get free.

'Please let me go! I'm not with you—I'm not one of you! Let me go!'

'Sophie!' Karl's bright glittering gaze mocked her struggles and the arm about her waist did not relax in the slightest, but rather held her more tightly as they entered the cable-car. 'Do not fight me so hard, little one, I am not going to hurt you!'

Little one—she remembered rather dazedly that he had called her that when he had known her three years ago, and she had thought it very charming and complimentary then. Now she felt it was rather patronising and she struggled anew against the steely arm about her waist.

'Let me go, Karl! I'm not coming with you, let me go!' She was squashed between several other bodies, some male, some female, and all of them tense and eager with excitement, smelling of cold air and expensive scents. 'Oh no!' She watched the doors closing and felt the car move, and her eyes were wide with dismay as she looked up at Karl. 'You—you had no right to make me come, you know——'

'That Flora will not like you being here also?' A fair brow mocked her wariness of Flora and he laughed, one gloved hand still resting with easy intimacy on her slender waist. 'It it time that you had some fun, little one; you spend too much time with Claude and not enough time with the big boys, eh?'

He laughed and it made her more uneasy than ever, apart from any dismay she felt about Flora's opinion. He smelled of some masculine scent that teased her nostrils and mingled tantalisingly with the warmth of his body, and she wished she had room to move away from that disturbingly intimate hand on her waist.

'I have a job to do, Karl, and you know Flora isn't going to like it when she finds me here.'

'You are afraid of her?'

The question was half amused, and she knew the woman immediately next to her was taking a cursory interest in what they were saying. It was impossible to carry on a conversation without being overheard by at least the three or four people nearest to them. After the clean coldness of the outside air the cable-car was overwhelmingly close and stuffy and filled with so many bodies that she felt much too hot.

'I'm not afraid of anyone.' She made the objection as quietly as possible, but even so the woman next to her was looking curiously at Karl, a fact that he seemed both unaware of and uncaring about. 'I just don't want to lose my job through something that isn't my fault, that's all. I'm not invited to this party, and I'm not in the habit of gate-crashing!'

'You are never invited, that is why I took the opportunity of whisking you away and giving you the chance to join in the fun.' He bent his head so that his voice breathed close to her ear and the warmth of his tanned cheek brushed hers, a contact that would have put her in the seventh heaven only three years ago. 'I do not think you are very grateful, Sophie, eh?'

'I'm grateful for the thought, Karl, but not for the fact that you didn't stop to think what Flora is going to say, or do, when she finds me here. She *is* my employer, you know.'

'But your cousin also, hmm?'

'My second cousin—it's not quite the same thing.'

'And are you not allowed to speak with anyone at all but little Claude? Does employing you give her the right to keep you confined to your room while we enjoy ourselves? You are too useful to her, little one! You must come out of your shell, it is not good that you hide yourself away so much.'

If only he knew, Sophie thought a little wildly; it was the only way she could keep her job, but not intruding on Flora's social life, and the job meant too much to her. Cousins they might be, but Flora would brook no bid for independence. Any stepping out of line would mean being sacked from the only job she was capable of doing—and besides, there was Claude.

'You—you don't understand, Karl!'

'I will try, if you tell me.'

The invitation was unmistakable, but Sophie was shaking her head. 'I don't want to talk about it, Karl, it doesn't concern anyone but me.'

'You do not believe anyone cares, eh?' A hint of impatience showed for a moment in his eyes as well as his voice, but she could not stand there and argue with him about the ethics of Flora's behaviour towards her; not with Flora's friends all around them.

'Please, Karl!'

His broad shoulders beneath a thick brown and red sweater shrugged impatiently. 'O.K.,' he said. 'But you will come this once because I have brought you, and you will leave Flora to me!'

There was nothing she could say, nowhere she could go, trapped as she was between him and the other people immediately surrounding them, so she simply stood rather stiffly and waited for the ride to end. They might have been suspended in outer space, for she could see nothing outside but the blue-black sky, as the small lighted car glided slowly up the mountain-side.

If only this had happened three years ago! That same echo kept going round and round in Sophie's brain, and the more she thought about it, the more helplessly angry she felt that it should have happened now. Now she could not afford to offend Flora, and Karl was not the be-all and end-all of her existence she had thought him then.

'I say, Karl, introduce me, won't you?' The voice was English and immediately behind her, and the warmth of his breath was on her neck, making her strain forward and away from it. 'I don't know the lady!'

Karl's hand still rested on her waist, and she felt the hard, strong fingers curve slightly more, digging into her, and at the same time the lean body that half supported her seemed to tense a little, as if he resented the intrusion. 'That is your loss, I am afraid, Ralph.' There was mockery in his voice but a hint of steel too that brought a swift reaction from her sensitive nerves. 'Sophie is with me.'

'Does Flora know?'

The jibe was deliberate and resentful, but the man laughed as if it had been intended as a joke. Sophie could imagine the look on Karl's face, she had seen it before. Narrow-eyed and glittering, a warning it was as well to heed, and the woman standing next to her had one brow raised curiously, her eyes flickering from Karl

to Sophie, sensing a situation that could prove interesting.

Sophie wanted to say something, to do something to
end the obvious misconception, but she could think of
nothing that would not make the situation even more
suspect. Nothing had been further from her mind when
she left the hotel to go for a walk than being whisked
away in a cable-car full of Flora's friends, with Karl's
hold on her firm and unyielding.

'No offence.'

The murmured effort at an apology mumbled past
her ear, and she felt Karl's fingers tighten their hold
momentarily, before easing slightly. Voices started up
again, covering the brief lull, and it was doubtful if the
majority of the party realised anything had been amiss.

A slight jolt sent her lurching against Karl, and then
the doors opened and the car stood at the steel and
concrete platform ready to disgorge its passengers.
Their immediate aim seemed to be the stark wood
and glass building where she and Claude had sat and
watched Karl speeding down towards the village from
the Maiden's Tower, and in the ensuing confusion
Sophie saw her chance.

She slipped away from that rather disturbingly possessive hand on her waist and lost herself among the
jostling bodies on the platform, ignoring Karl's voice
calling after her and seeking the concealment of the
shadows around the towering columns at the far end,
before he could make his way out of the car.

Chilled by the sudden biting cold of isolation, she
stood for a moment wondering what on earth she had
hoped to achieve by the manoeuvre, when there was no
way down from the vastness of the snowy massif except
the way she had come. And she could hardly hope to

achieve that without Karl spotting her.

She stood behind one of the support columns feeling faintly ridiculous, for in all probability Karl would not even bother to look for her. Also she was a free agent, able to do as she pleased. All she had to do was to wait for the car to make the return journey and go down with it; nevertheless, for the time being, she stayed where she was.

All hope of his not bothering to look for her was banished when the last of the crowd made their way into the restaurant, for Karl still stood in the doorway of the car looking around for her, with his brows drawn into a frown. Then Flora's voice called to him from the restaurant and she came and stood in the door, her golden hair gleaming in the bright lights and one hand signalling to him to come and join her.

'Aren't you coming in, darling?' She came further out into the cold air and shivered. 'Oh, do come on, Karl darling, it's so cold! What are you hanging about out here for?'

Sophie, from her concealment, heard him laugh shortly as he heaved his long lean body away from the supporting door frame. 'God knows,' he said in a flat voice. 'It seems I have been made a fool of by——' His broad shoulders shrugged carelessly, while Sophie held her breath, hoping he was not going to betray the fact that she was there somewhere.

'Darling?' Flora put a possessive arm through his and pulled her slender body close to him, looking up into the shadowed face curiously. 'Who *did* you come with? I looked for you in the first car, but you waited until the last one. Why?'

Whether or not he resented the interrogation, Sophie could not be sure, but it was clear that he did not like facing the fact that she, Sophie, had not been duly grateful to him for bringing her to the party. He stood for a moment in shadow of the covered platform, near the restaurant door, then once more shrugged his shoulders.

'I do not know; I was a fool, I suppose; but I thought I knew women.'

'Oh, but you do, darling!' Flora raised herself on tip-toe and kissed him. 'Far too many of them for my liking! Now come and join the party or I shall be sorry I brought you all up here.'

If only they *would* go in, Sophie thought, for the attendant was already turning the car in preparation for the return journey, and she wanted to go with it, but not at the risk of Flora seeing her. Maybe she was idiotic to care so much, but at the moment Flora was unmistakably jealous because she knew Karl had come up with someone else instead of her. If she discovered who it was she would be doubly furious, and Sophie was bound to be the loser.

'Karl?' Flora's voice was soft and coaxing, nothing like the shrill weapon she was capable of producing when she dealt with Sophie or even her own son, and she gazed up at him with her blue eyes pleading. 'Come and join the party, please.'

It was a second or two before Karl eventually consented. He took a last look around, then shrugged his broad shoulders and turned into the restaurant doors with Flora's arm tucked through his, but by then the cable-car was already on its way down again, and Sophie watched it go, sighing her exasperation. There was nothing she could do now but wait for the next car and she could hardly wait inside and give away what she had gone to so much trouble to conceal.

It was bitterly cold, but she stayed out of the wind as much as possible, hugging her arms about her body in an effort to keep warm. It was light enough, except under the shadowy beams that helped to support the working party of the cable system, and she gazed at the lighted windows of the restaurant with envy, her eyes instinctively seeking out Karl's tall figure.

When temptation threatened to become too much for her, she turned her back on the warm crowded restaurant, resolutely refusing to succumb, and hugged herself more tightly. She had stood like that for several minutes when she heard footsteps on the concrete plat-form behind her and turned swiftly to see who it was.

The man was a stranger to her, but his voice when he spoke was familiar, and she recognised the English pas-senger, Ralph, whom Karl had so thoroughly snubbed when he asked to be introduced. He was fairly short, which would account for why his voice had sounded so close to her ear, and he had a huge moustache which aged a somewhat boyish face and also helped to disguise a rather weak mouth and chin.

He was smiling and as he came towards her his intention was obvious. In one hand he carried a large glass of brandy which he held out in front of him, waving it to and fro as a tempting bait. 'No drink?' he asked, trying to put the brandy glass into her hand. 'And what are you doing out here in the cold, eh?'

He had pale-coloured eyes and his hair was light too, also it was obvious that he had already had far too much to drink. He was an unprepossessing figure, though he seemed to expect her to be glad to see him.

'I know,' he guessed with a laugh, 'you thought I'd come and find you, didn't you?'

Sophie wished he would go. She had no fear of him,

but he could be the cause of others coming outside, and she did not want to be discovered now that she was so close to getting back down. The way the cables were vibrating told her that there was a car on its way up and she looked anxiously beyond the man who smiled so invitingly at her.

'I'm on my way down,' she told him firmly. 'And I don't want a drink, thank you.'

'Oh, nonsense, of course you do!' He looked back at the bright interior of the restaurant and laughed. 'Have you and the sexy Swiss had a fight?' he asked. 'Just as well, you know; Flora would have had your eyes if she'd caught you with him!'

Sophie said nothing. She hoped that if she ignored him he would be discouraged and leave her alone again, but he was less easily deterred than she hoped, and the thought of her having evaded Karl seemed to delight him; he was laughing again.

'I'll bet he's fuming, isn't he? It's not often the great Bruner gets the brush-off, I'll bet his ego's suffering!' The glass of brandy was waved under her nose once more. 'Have a little drink, love, while you're waiting. Keep you warm.'

'No, thank you!'

She spoke firmly, but she was beginning to realise that he had no intention of leaving her, and she watched anxiously for the arrival of the cable-car. A hand on her arm made her jerk back swiftly and she stepped away from him, coming up against the solid barrier of the column. He followed, trying to press the glass into her hand and smiling at her vaguely.

'Oh, come on, it's a party!'

'No!'

He put a hand on the column behind her and leaned

closer. His face was close to hers and the brandy glass
wavered unsteadily in front of her lips, as if he meant
to force her to drink, so that Sophie turned her head
jerkily from side to side as she made an attempt to duck
under his arm.

She had seen no one else approach, but a large hand
reached over suddenly and took the brandy glass, setting it down on one of the concrete beams, and she saw
Karl's tanned face and narrowed eyes over the man's
shoulder. He was smiling, but there was no glimmer of
humour in the icy blueness of his eyes.

'You will go inside and leave the young lady alone,
Ralph.' His voice was quiet, deep and authoritative
with just that barely perceptible accent, and the man
resented it as much as he had in the cable-car coming
up.

'*You* go back inside!' he advised slurrily. 'You're not
wanted out here!'

Briefly Karl flicked Sophie a glance. 'Neither are you,
I think. Please go back inside with the others.' The man
looked like arguing further, but before he could say
a word Karl took his arm and turned him round to
face the door of the restaurant. 'If you do not I shall
be obliged to hit you,' Karl went on in the same cool
firm voice, 'and I do not like to cause incidents that
can be embarrassing to both you and the lady.'

For a second the man wavered. From his face it was
obvious he hated backing down, but he lacked the
necessary courage to make an issue of Karl's right to
interfere for the moment. His face was flushed and he
looked spiteful in the way that a child does, and he half
turned as he held on to a column for support.

'Damn you, Bruner! What gives you the right to
interfere?'

Karl's mouth was twitching at one corner and there was a bright and slightly malicious glimmer of laughter in his eyes. 'I am an old friend, a very old friend of both Miss Roberts and her father; is that not true, Sophie?'

'Yes.'

Her voice was scarcely more than a whisper, but she did not see how she could deny it. He had been a friend in the old days, to her father as well as to her, and nothing had happened between them since to make it any different. It was not an easy thing to admit, but she thought it possible that he saw her still as an eighteen-year-old girl. It did not occur to him that she was now a grown woman and able to take care of herself.

A firm hand grasped her shoulder with the same disturbing suggestion of possessiveness she had noticed earlier, and it seemed to be confirmation enough for the other man. The doors closed behind him and only then did Karl turn and really look at her, his eyes bright and curious in the shadowy darkness.

He too was bare-headed and his fair hair looked almost as golden as Flora's, though there was nothing artificial about his colouring. He did not smile, but his mouth showed a slight quiver that suggested he found some amusement in the situation.

'Why are you hiding out here, you silly little creature?' He asked the question softly, and Sophie flushed at the names he used. 'You do not have to fear Flora *so* much, surely. Come inside and drink something to warm you.' Taking both her hands in his, he stood looking down at her. 'You must be almost frozen standing here.'

'I am cold.' She admitted it without hesitation, but glanced at the tell-tale vibration of the cable and shook her head. 'But the car's on its way up and I'll be back in the hotel before very long.'

'In the meantime you will determinedly suffer in the cold, eh?' There was an edge of impatience on his voice, and she realised how easily he seemed to lose patience with her. Or perhaps he always had and she had simply not noticed it. 'Are you so afraid of facing Flora, Sophie?'

'I'd rather *not* face her, it isn't a case of being afraid.' She made the denial firmly, determined not to be considered a coward and too frightened of Flora to have a mind of her own. 'It's a matter of policy. She wouldn't like me joining her party uninvited, and I don't want to risk my job by offending her; it's as simple as that.'

'This—job is so important to you?'

It struck her suddenly that he probably had no idea of her situation, for there was no real reason why he should. The financial follies of an ordinary business man were not of the same world-shattering importance as Flora's divorce, and Flora was unlikely to have spared time to explain it to him.

It was not an easy subject to raise, but somehow she felt that in the circumstances Karl had some right to know at least a little about her position, and why it was so important for her to keep on the right side of Flora.

'I—I have to work, Karl, and this job—this kind of job is the only work I'm fitted for. Looking after Claude is the only talent I have and I was very grateful to Flora when she took me on. I can't *afford* to offend her.'

'It came to that?' His sympathy was almost unbearable and she stiffened her small figure against the inclination she had to put her head against his shoulder. 'I did not realise this, Sophie. Your poor father was not such a good business head, eh?'

'No.' She shook her head, not looking up at him for the moment. 'But I'm quite happy with Flora; looking after Claude isn't hard and I travel around a lot with them.'

Glancing over his shoulder he smiled grimly. 'And knowing Flora it is not easy either,' he said. 'What is there I can do to help, Sophie?'

'Oh, nothing, really!' The suggestion took her by surprise and she shrank from the idea of his feeling sorry for her to such an extent that he wanted to help. 'I like what I do, and I've no desire to do anything else. I love little Claude and he likes me, we get along fine, better than I'd dared hope when I started with them.'

'But you are beholden to Flora, and that is not good, I think.'

She wished fervently that the cable-car would hurry and arrive, for she found the conversation more embarrassing than she would have believed possible. The cables hummed and shivered in the cold air and the dark gliding shape of the car came into view below them, suspended over the snowy slopes.

'I really don't mind.' She was so anxious to convince him that she almost convinced herself. 'And at least Flora is family.'

The full significance of what she implied did not strike her until the car slid alongside where they stood and she saw Karl's face more clearly in the lights from its windows. He took it that she would far rather be beholden to Flora, because she was family, no matter how unpleasantly she treated her, than to him, and his firm, tight mouth showed how much he resented it.

'Of course,' he said stiffly. 'I understand.'

'Oh, Karl, I didn't mean——' She bit her lip hastily, seeking ways of apologising for the unintended slight.

'There isn't anything you could do to help, although I—I'm very grateful to you for wanting to.'

'But you will not *let* me help?'

Temptation as well as curiosity prompted her when she looked up at him, and there was a small flutter of hope in her heart. '*Could* you?'

He laughed, and his laughter echoed round the bare concrete walls bringing a sudden warmth to her spirit, as the big hands holding her gloved fingers warmed her flesh.

'I will see what I can do,' he promised. 'I think you will be surprised.'

'Karl——'

'Goodnight, little one!'

He bent his head swiftly and kissed her mouth, and Sophie was so unprepared for it that she simply allowed him to push her into the now empty car with a large hand at her back, and when she turned and looked back, just before the doors slid together, he was smiling. The gesture of putting a hand to touch her lips was purely instinctive, but she recovered sufficiently to wave a hand as the car started on its return journey— and she thanked heaven Flora had not seen that brief but completely unexpected salute.

CHAPTER THREE

SOPHIE had no idea what to expect from Karl in the way of help, or even if she should expect anything at all. The atmosphere on the dizzying heights of the Schillenberg that night had been charged with emotion, and he could simply have been affected by it and spoken without thinking, however serious he had seemed at the time. It was two days now since he had virtually taken her by force to join Flora's party, and she had heard nothing more from him as yet.

She sat with Claude on the balcony terrace of the hotel restaurant having coffee, and for the moment they were alone. Not that there was anything unusual in that, but she had seen Robert St John for a few moments last evening, and he had promised to join them for coffee. The fact that he had not so far put in an appearance was not entirely unexpected either, for he was pretty much involved with Flora.

Flora still made it quite clear that Karl held her main interest, but Robert seemed satisfied to simply be allowed to join her retinue, and his attitude sometimes irritated Sophie. Karl would put in an appearance whenever he felt like it and he was not engaged in practice on the slopes, but he never just became one of the crowd. He joined them because they amused him; sometimes Sophie suspected he despised them, but Robert was in awe of the bright, brittle glamour that surrounded Flora, and Sophie was a little disappointed at his willingness to become a conquest.

'Mr St John is coming.'

Claude's voice brought her out of her reverie, and she looked over her shoulder to see Robert striding in their direction with a brisk confident stride she had never noticed before. He was wearing ski-boots and the inevitable windproof jacket, and there was a fresh-faced look about him that suggested he had been trying out his injured legs on the slopes this morning.

Dropping on to a chair beside her, he smiled as apologetically as his obvious satisfaction allowed. 'Good morning—did you think I'd forgotten our date?'

'No, not really.' She could see he was beamingly pleased about something and guessed that his first venture had gone well. 'Have you been on the slopes?' He nodded, unable to restrain a grin of pleasure. 'How did it go?'

'Marvellously! I felt no twinges at all; just a bit of stiffness in one knee, that's all, but nothing as bad as I expected.' He laughed, delighted with his progress, and winked an eye at Claude, who was looking at him with the usual envy in his eyes. 'St Moritz, here I come, eh, Claude?'

'You think you'll be ready for the championships?'

It seemed such a short time before the big event, but Robert seemed so confident that she wondered if perhaps she should have concealed her doubts. 'I hope so.' Once more he flicked a glance at Claude. 'Of course I'll have Karl Bruner to beat, but—I have hopes.'

'Karl will win!'

Claude had no doubts at all about his hero's ability, and he saw no reason to be polite about saying so—a fact that Robert acknowledged with a wry smile. 'I'll just have to be that little bit better, then, won't I?'

'For England!' Sophie waved an imaginary flag, and Robert laughed.

'If only I hadn't to beat him on his own ground!'

Sophie thought of Karl's tall, lean body skimming like a bird down the snowy slopes and wondered if it really could make so much difference. He was equally proficient wherever he skied; Austria, America or wherever international competitions took place, and it seemed a little unfair to suggest that Switzerland gave him much of an advantage.

'Does that make such a difference to a top-grade skier?' she asked, and something in her voice made Robert give her a slightly narrowed look before shaking his head.

'I suppose it shouldn't,' he allowed. 'And of course you'll be cheering for him, won't you, Sophie?'

He somehow managed to make it sound like an accusation, and Sophie felt herself flushing as she shook her head. The ego of any international sporting star was a very touchy thing, and she should not let Robert think he did not have the support of his own countrywoman.

'I shall be cheering for you,' she told him with a smile. 'How could I do anything else?'

'Good!' He winked an eye once more at Claude, and laughed. 'And what about you, Claude?'

'I shall want Karl to win,' Claude told him without hesitation, 'because he is going to be my father.'

His insistence that Karl was going to become his stepfather was becoming increasingly embarrassing, but Sophie could not see how on earth she was going to stop him. He liked Karl and admired him and that, combined with his mother's unconcealed determination, was enough for him. Robert, however, saw less reason to conceal his curiosity about it, and Sophie suspected it was prompted in no small way by jealousy, not only of Karl's prowess as a skier, but of his success with Flora as well.

'You sound pretty sure about that,' he said to the boy. 'What makes you think Karl Bruner is going to be your stepfather, Claude?'

It took the boy a moment or two to sort out exactly what it was he was being asked, but then he looked at Robert solemnly and shook his head. 'I want him to be,' he stated, as if that was reason enough, 'and so does Maman.'

'Oh, I see.' Robert caught Sophie's eye and it was clear that he did not like the answer. 'Well, wouldn't it be a better idea to wait until your *maman* or Karl Bruner make it official before you tell anybody else?'

Claude nodded but he was so obviously puzzled by the reasoning that Sophie instinctively reached for his hand. She was very fond of her small charge and she did her best to see that he was happy. If he thought there was any doubt that Karl was going to be his stepfather he would be very upset—and so too would Flora, she thought ruefully.

'I don't think Claude's likely to tell anyone else about it, are you, Claude?' She smiled down at him and brushed back the dark hair from his forehead. 'You know how to keep a secret, don't you?'

'Why?'

In sudden helplessness Sophie looked across at Robert, then licked her lips anxiously before venturing to provide an answer herself. 'It's—well, it isn't a very good idea to tell everyone about something that—well, that might not happen. Do you understand what I mean, Claude?'

Claude nodded, but it was clear that he neither believed Karl was not to be his father, nor that he saw any reason to conceal his pride in the fact. He held his coffee cup between both his hands and drank some of it while he thought over what she had said, then he put it down carefully with the obvious intention of questioning her further; but at that moment Flora joined them.

As usual she almost completely ignored him and Sophie, except to acknowledge their presence with a slight nod, but it was too commonplace an occurrence to trouble Claude, and he remained quiet while his mother gave her attention to Robert.

'Oh, *there* you are!' Her bright head was without a hat and it gleamed like gold in the sunlight as she smiled at Robert getting to his feet. 'Bobby darling, are you going to be *very* occupied this morning?'

It would not matter if he had to practise, Sophie realised with a twinge of impatience, he was ready to do anything. He would almost certainly have spent some more time on the slopes after his break with her and Claude, but if Flora claimed him he would willingly forgo his badly needed practice to please her.

'It isn't anything I can't leave for a few minutes to do something for you, Flora, you know that. What is it you want?'

Flora was wearing what Sophie designated her little girl look, although there was nothing childish about those bright eyes and finely chiselled features. But her mouth was pouted slightly and she looked hard done by as she put both hands to the collar of her bright green parka and pushed the soft fur up under her chin, looking at Robert through her lashes.

'Am I being selfish?'

'Good lord, of course not!'

Sophie watched the play with a sense of resignation; she had seen it all before, and it left her feeling rather saddened. Robert was a talented man and well able to hold his own in most circumstances, but when it came to Flora he was completely blind. As for Claude, he was giving all his attention to the view from the balcony. The mountains and the ski-runs—indulging in his favourite daydreams—he had seen it all before too.

Flora was smiling and tucking her arm through Robert's with the same possessive air of intimacy that Sophie had noticed her use towards Karl only two nights ago. Whatever Robert's plans had been, it was inevitable that he would fall in with whatever Flora wanted to do, and they both knew it.

'I'd planned to go down into Schatzheim and do some shopping,' she told him plaintively, 'but there's no one to drive me.'

'To Schatzheim?'

Sophie saw his expression when he repeated the name; Schatzheim was some fifty kilometres away, but she saw the hasty recovery he made too. Flora, she thought, had spotted it too, and anticipated a change of mind.

'Darling, you're not going to disappoint me too, are you?'

Obviously she had had someone else in mind originally, and Sophie had little doubt who it was. Robert knew it too, though he did his best to ignore it, she guessed, as he hastened to reassure her.

'I wouldn't dream of disappointing you, Flora!'

'I knew you wouldn't, Bobby darling, you're much too good to me!'

Flora tip toed and kissed him lightly on his forehead, her smile brightly satisfied as she looked at his slightly dazed expression. But he had not anticipated a trip that could take up most of the day, Sophie thought, even though he did his best to put a good face on it.

There was no doubt at all that Karl had been Flora's original choice to escort her, but Karl was not the type of man to let anything or anyone come between him and the chance of the championship—he was far too single-minded for that. Flattered as he might be, Sophie could see that Robert was already regretting the time he was going to lose, though possibly he would count it well worth while for the moment.

He had for the moment forgotten that he was there to have coffee with Sophie and Claude, but catching her eye reminded him and he looked embarrassed and un-easy as he swiftly avoided her gaze and looked instead at Flora.

'I was—I mean, I'd arranged to have coffee with Sophie and Claude this morning, Flora. If you could——'

'Oh, for heaven's sake, Bobby dear, they won't mind!' She dismissed the importance of any previous arrangement with an airy hand—especially one that involved her son and his nursemaid. She laughed and stroked one slim forefinger down the sleeve of his jacket, looking up at him with a slight curl on her lower lip, her eyes half hidden. 'Of course, Bobby, if you'd rather not come, I could——'

'Oh, but of course I want to take you, Flora! I won't take a minute to change.'

'There's no need to change, darling, you look quite gorgeous the way you are.'

To Sophie's astonishment Robert blushed like a schoolboy; he was very conscious of the little boy sitting there, she thought, and felt vaguely sorry for him. 'I'll have to change my boots,' he insisted. 'It won't take me very long, Flora. Why don't you wait here with Sophie and Claude and have a coffee to keep out the cold?'

Flora sighed; resigned to being kept waiting, but not to being left in the company of her son and Sophie. 'If you must, Bobby darling. But I'd much rather wait in the bar for you; it's cosier in there and I can chat to someone while I'm waiting.'

There was a hint of threat in that last, Sophie recognised, and had no doubt that Robert did too; Flora did not miss a trick when it came to holding the whip hand. The glance Robert gave Sophie was half apologetic and half defensive, and she despaired of his readiness to fall in with Flora's plans, even when he knew she was making use of him.

'Sophie——'

'Don't be too long, Bobby, will you?'

'No, no, I'll just have a word with Sophie.' He looked at her appealingly, and once more she felt impatience stirring in her. 'I'm sorry about the coffee, Sophie, I did promise, I know, but—maybe tomorrow, hmm?'

'Yes, of course.'

She found it too hard to smile and be normally pleasant when she said it, because she felt so annoyed with him. Not only because he was letting her and Claude down, but because he was making himself such a willing pawn in Flora's game of trying to rouse Karl's jealousy. She knew it troubled him too, that he was ully aware that he was being made use of, and yet he did nothing about it.

'You do understand?'

Sophie smiled wryly. 'Oh yes, perfectly!'

'I really am sorry, Sophie.'

Flora had already left them and was making her way back across the terrace, her tall, thin shape carelessly confident, not even looking back to see whether or not Robert was following her; and Sophie watched her for a second or two, aware of Robert's anxious glance flitting between the two of them. Then she looked up at him and smiled.

'Oh, just don't worry about it, Robert, it really doesn't matter in the least. And I think you'd better go, or you might just find someone else has been appointed in your place!' She had not meant to sound quite so malicious and she sought to make amends, shaking her head and laughing. 'Actually you're probably well out of it; we shall very likely do as we most always do—ride up to the Maiden's Tower and watch the skiers.'

His gaze went briefly to the snowy vastness of the mountains and he allowed his regret to show in his eyes for a moment. 'I expect you'll find Karl Bruner out there,' he said. 'He went off early this morning, before I did, and he's still out.' A wry smile crossed his face briefly. 'He means to beat me again this time!'

Sophie said nothing to suggest otherwise, but merely smiled. 'Have fun on your trip, Robert.'

He hesitated only a second longer, then glanced over at Flora just disappearing into the hotel. 'Thanks,' he said, and hurried after her.

As Sophie expected, Claude's sole interest was to ride

up to the Maiden's Tower by cable-car and then sit
and watch the skiing from the restaurant windows. It
was his favourite occupation at the moment, and
Sophie saw no harm in indulging him for the time being. Sooner or later the novelty would doubtless fade,
and then he would want to do something else instead.

She had dressed him in his new ski-suit, blue with a
red stripe down the legs of the trousers, just like the
one Karl wore, and his usual red hat pulled on snugly
under the hood of his jacket. He always looked so
cutely cuddly when he was dressed up in so many thick
garments that she never could resist giving him a hug,
and he accepted it, usually with a giggle.

She had nothing new herself. The money Flora paid
her did not run to many new clothes, but her wardrobe
had been well stocked during her father's lifetime, and
it was still quite good enough. A cinnamon brown
jacket and trousers with a pale fur trimming, and
brown boots, were warm as well as complementary to
her colouring, and she had a small knitted hat in dark
yellow that went with it.

Claude was waiting impatiently for her, and she took
a last hasty look in the mirror, then went to join him,
turning to close the door behind them. Reaching down
for Claude's hand, she glanced up quickly when he
darted away from her and ran along the corridor towards the stairway, calling out as he went.

'Karl! Karl! Why are you here? I was going to watch
you ski—now you are here and I cannot watch you!'

Knowing Karl's room was on the floor below, Sophie
guessed he had come in search of Flora, and she wished
she did not feel quite so glad of the opportunity to tell
him that Flora was already on her way to Schatzheim
with Robert.

He wore the ski-suit.that Claude had demanded a miniature duplicate of, and he towered over the little figure beside him while he looked along the corridor, waiting for Sophie to join them. He had the same fresh-faced, open-air look that Robert had had and from the same cause, and he seemed to glow with good health and a startling air of earthy virility. His head was bare, his thick hair rumpled and untidy where it had been confined to a cap that had been hastily snatched off, and his blue eyes were stunningly bright in a tanned face.

'I am glad that I caught you.' He said nothing until she came within hearing, but she noticed how he had taken Claude's hand in his. He always had that natural, easy way with children, she had noticed it before and thought how at odds it was with his reputation as a woman's man. 'Do you particularly wish to go to the Mädchen Turm again?'

He was not concerned with Claude's choice, but hers, and Sophie shook her head a little dazedly, wondering why it should concern him. 'Claude likes to go, that's the only reason we go so often. He likes to watch you practise.'

A wide grin split the tanned face with strong even teeth, and he looked down at his small admirer teasingly. 'I have done as much practice as I intend to do this morning,' he told him. 'I have something else in mind for the rest of the day.' He glanced beyond Sophie and along the corridor. 'Where is your *maman?*'

So he *was* in search of Flora, Sophie thought, and wondered why she felt so angry suddenly. Speaking up hastily, she forestalled Claude's reply. 'Flora's out. She went into Schatzheim with Robert, about twenty minutes ago.' She tried to do something about the satisfaction in her voice but did not manage it. 'If you drive fast enough I expect you could catch them!'

Brows raised, Karl looked at her for a moment curiously, then he smiled slowly and with such unmistakable meaning that she felt a flush warm her cheeks. 'I was hoping that I could persuade her to behave like a mother for once in her life,' he told her quietly, 'and take care of Claude while I took you on a visit, Sophie. But since that is not possible, then Claude must come too.'

'A visit?' She was not quite sure whether or not to believe it at the moment, but Claude was in no doubt about how he felt. He would go anywhere with Karl, whether he had been intended to or not. 'Karl, I——'

'We can go, we can go, we can go!'

Claude chanted the words loud and long enough to drown what she had been going to say, and Karl placed a large but gentle hand over his mouth and frowned at him in mock anger. 'You will go nowhere unless you behave,' he told him sternly. 'It is if Sophie wishes to come that counts.' He returned his gaze to her and she found it very hard to meet his eyes. 'Will you come, Sophie?'

She nodded silently at first, and could not understand why he looked quite so pleased. 'Yes, of course. Thank you, Karl, we'd like to go—wherever it is you have in mind.' She laughed a little unsteadily and put both hands to her yellow hat to pull it further down over her ears. 'I don't remember the last time I went on a mystery outing.'

'Now?' Claude was insistent, and Karl looked down at him and sighed resignedly.

'Now,' he agreed patiently. 'If Sophie is ready to go now.'

'Am I?' She looked down at the clothes she wore and

laughed. 'I don't know how I'm supposed to dress for this trip.'

'Like you are is just perfect,' Karl said in his quiet voice, and let go Claude's hand to look at the watch on his wrist. 'I will take about five minutes to change; will you wait for me downstairs?'

'Yes, of course.'

He held her uncertain gaze for a moment, then smiled slowly. 'Good,' he said softly. 'I will be very quick!'

In fact it was a little more than ten minutes before Karl joined them in the hotel foyer, and Sophie was surprised to realise that she was actually anxious after the allotted five minutes were gone. She had no need to be, she told herself, for Karl was not going to be waylaid by Flora. Flora was safely out of the way, on her way to Schatzheim with Robert. It did not yet occur to her to worry about what Flora was likely to say if she discovered Karl was somewhere with Sophie, while she had had to make do with Robert's company.

When Karl did come the ski-suit had been exchanged for a pair of close-fitting blue trousers and a thick white sweater under a bulky, fur-lined jacket, and the ski-boots for soft suede ones in dark brown to match the jacket. His head was still bare, but he had tidied his hair by brushing it back from his forehead and making an attempt to straighten its inclination to curl just above his brow.

Claude wriggled down from his seat when he saw him coming and ran across the foyer to meet him, skipping along with his own small hand completely encompassed by Karl's strong brown fingers. 'Have I been very long?' he asked in such a way that she knew he did not mean it

as an apology. 'I stopped to make a phone call.' Looking
down at Claude, he pulled a face. 'I had to let them
know that there would be one more than I had said
for lunch.'

'Oh, I see.'

Sophie could not imagine where they could be going.
It sounded very much as if it might be a private home
if forewarning was needed of an extra guest, and she
wondered where on earth he was taking them. Claude
was unconcerned, wherever it might be, he was simply
excited to be going anywhere with the man he was so
sure was going to be his stepfather.

That was something that nagged at the back of
Sophie's mind as they walked out to the car. What the
actual position was between Flora and Karl, she did not
know, but somehow she did not think it was as settled
as Flora wanted it to be. Claude's habit of referring to
him as soon to be his father might prove very embarrassing in some circumstances if that was so, and she
hoped Karl was up to dealing with it, for she was
certain she was not.

It was warm in the car and they dispensed with hats
and gloves while Karl drove them up and around the
long, tortuous road from Brunnenheim. Mountain
roads were often impassable at this time of year, but so
far they had met no difficulties, and Sophie was more
than ever sure that they must be going to visit a private
home, for he would surely not drive them such a route
otherwise.

'Have you seen the valley from here before?'

He was sure she had not, and the pleasure he took in
pointing out such a breathtaking view showed his pride
in his country. It was an understandable pride, for

every new turn and twist in the snake-like road revealed another stunning view.

The towering dominance of the Schillenberg was to
their right and it glittered like a huge diamond in the
sunlight, with its ragged circlet of pines like a dark line
drawn around it. The scattered houses below in the
valley looked like toys surrounded by Christmas trees,
and long sweeping ski-runs dotted with fast moving
figures, skirting a gully or taking a steep piste, like
animated dolls.

Being so high up and able to see so far gave Sophie
a curious sense of detachment, not unlike the sensation
she got looking down from the height of the Maiden's
Tower. She sometimes felt almost god-like, gazing at
the endless vista of snow and trees and tiny houses, and
the scene never seemed to pall because it was constantly
changing.

'It looks beautiful from here.'

'It *is* beautiful, hmm?'

The brief glance he gave over his shoulder took his
mind off his driving for only a second, and he firmly
corrected a very slight drift of the car on the curving
road between its banks of snow. Even so Sophie's
stomach experienced another fluttering thrill, and she
caught the handle beside her instinctively and held on
tightly.

'We're very high up now, aren't we?'

'Not so very high.' Karl's smile teased her, and she was
confident he knew all about that disturbing sensation
in her stomach. 'You are not frightened, are you,
Sophie?'

'No, of course I'm not frightened!'

She denied it hastily, for Claude would have been

most surprised if she had admitted to being nervous. He had absolutely no fear of anything to do with the mountains, and he could not understand anyone who had. He had the back seat of the car to himself, and inevitably he had his nose pressed to the window as he watched the skiers in the valley, fascinated as always. He would, Sophie guessed ruefully, have been content to go on climbing for ever; the steep, snow-banked road held no terrors for him.

Then suddenly they were caught in one of those unexpectedly magical moments that seem to happen so often in the Alps—another turn in the road and they were in a small village. Even smaller than Brunnenheim, it was obviously not a tourist centre, for there were no cable-cars and not even a ski-lift and, so far as Sophie could see, only one hotel. After the bustling liveliness of Brunnenheim it seemed very quiet and remote, but quite incredibly beautiful set among the lesser peaks, with its houses crowded in by towering pines.

'This is lovely, Karl!' She looked at him expectantly, for some instinct told her that this was their destination, even before he confirmed it. 'What is it called?'

'Schläfing—you will not have heard of it, I think.'

'I haven't, but it's beautiful.' She watched the half-smile on his mouth curiously. 'Is it somewhere special?'

'To me it is special.' There were no gardens in front of the houses, only large open spaces set amid snow-covered bushes and trees, and Karl took the car on to one of these, then drove without pause down a sloping ramp into a partially underground garage. Switching off the engine, he smiled at her briefly. 'Some of my family live here.'

'Oh. Oh, I see.'

He got out and came round to open the door for her, smiling as he handed her from the car. 'Are you curious, Sophie?'

Catching sight of that half-smile, she looked up at him challengingly. 'Yes, of course I'm curious—you expected me to be, didn't you, Karl?'

'Huh-huh.' Another brief smile recognised the challenge and found it amusing, but he did nothing more to enlighten her, only turned to help Claude from the back seat. 'Shall we go and meet our hostess?'

Karl took his hand and Claude walked along beside him quite happily; anything Karl chose to do was all right with Claude. The other large hand slipped beneath Sophie's arm and took her along as they walked out into the clean coldness of outdoors again.

The house was built in the traditional chalet design, but it was huge and white, its windows framed in bright green shutters that were set open to the sunshine, and a steep flight of steps led to the front door. The customary wide-angled roof sloped almost to the ground one side and for all its size it had the same quaintly dolls' house appearance that the smaller houses in the village had.

They were still some distance from the steps when the door was flung open and two small boys came running out, skipping down the steps in such haste they seemed likely to fall. Shouting as they came, something in German-Swiss that Sophie could not understand, they came without hesitation and hurled themselves at Karl, dancing with excitement.

Both were blond and blue-eyed, and the elder one looked to be about six years old, the younger one about the same age as Claude, between four and five. There was such a marked resemblance to Karl that there could be no doubt they were his family, and they quite obviously adored him.

A murmured appeal in their own tongue quieted them and they gave their attention to their other visitors, giving special attention to Claude. As always, Claude was a little wary. He was far more used to adults than other children and he took a while to get used to them. Karl, however, took it upon himself to introduce them and he turned the children first to face her, making introductions in English.

'Sophie, I would like you to meet Hugo and Johann, Hans to us; boys, this is Miss Roberts from England, and we will speak English to her, eh?'

Two blond heads nodded obediently and two small hands were stretched out a trifle self-consciously for her to shake. It was all very solemn and serious, and Sophie gave them each an encouraging smile as she shook hands with them.

'Fräulein Roberts, I am pleased to meet you.'

'*Miss* Roberts, if you please, Hugo.'

Karl made the correction quietly, and the boy bobbed a brief apology. 'Miss Roberts.'

The younger boy contented himself with a handshake and a nod, he was far more interested in Claude, and the two of them stood looking at one another for a second or two before Karl introduced them to one another. 'And this is Claude Dauzan; Hugo and Hans Bruner.' Even the name was the same, Sophie noted, and looked up when Karl took her arm again, seeing a small, half-teasing smile that she found oddly discomfiting, as if he suspected her conclusions were less than charitable. 'Shall we go and meet their mother?' he suggested.

Inside, the house was far more luxurious than even

its vast exterior led one to expect, and a glossily polished wood floor gleamed like a mirror where its surface was not covered with deep pile rugs. Wide and low-ceilinged, the entrance hall was panelled with pine boards, mellowed to a deep golden colour and hung with banners and pennants and the occasional painting of mountains and country scenes.

It was warm, especially so after the cold air outside, and as they stepped inside, another door opened across the other side of the hall and a young woman came out, hastily removing an apron. She was flushed and smiling and in an advanced state of pregnancy—she was also extremely pretty and obviously glad to see Karl, whatever his relationship to her.

'*Mein lieber* Karl!' He kissed her soundly and she laughed when he held her away from him and studied her sparkling eyes and flushed cheeks. 'I have been in the kitchen helping Hilde; you know I cannot resist to cook!'

'And Anton is away!' Karl shook his head at her in mock reproach, then turned to introduce her to Sophie. 'I have brought Sophie to see you, as I promised, you see. Miss Sophie Roberts; my sister-in-law, Lisa.'

'I am most glad to welcome you!' Both Sophie's hands were taken in a warm clasp, and the woman's blue eyes smiled a welcome. It was clear that she was very glad to see her, and Sophie wondered a little uneasily on just what footing Karl had put their relationship when he spoke of her. 'You have met my boys?' Lisa Bruner looked at her anxiously, and Sophie nodded.

'Oh yes, we met outside when we arrived. They're lovely boys, and charmingly polite.'

Lisa nodded. 'Oh yes, Anton would not have them

other than polite,' she insisted, presumably referring to her husband. 'But they are friendly boys, yes?'

She seemed quite astonishingly anxious for Sophie to approve of her sons and at the moment she found it a little puzzling. 'Very friendly,' she agreed. 'I have a soft spot for little boys.'

'You like them?' Sophie nodded. 'Ah, that is good!'

Surprisingly Claude seemed to have made his own friends, and he was standing with the two blond Bruner boys telling them of the skiers he had seen in the valley on their way there. Apparently they shared a mutual passion for skiing, and with a resigned shrug Lisa Bruner led the way across the hall.

'The children will play,' she suggested. 'While we talk, eh?' She smiled up at her brother-in-law as he walked between the two of them and raised her brows. 'There is much to talk about, is there not, Karl?'

They walked into the main living room as she asked the question, but all else was banished from Sophie's mind by the sheer breathtaking vastness of the view. Her reaction was not unexpected, she thought, and Lisa smilingly led her to chairs set in a huge picture window that overlooked a magnificent panorama of mountains and valleys. A window like this was completely out of character with the traditional front of the house, but nothing else could have done credit to the view.

The floor here was in polished wood too, scattered with luxurious rugs as the entrance hall was, and the armchairs were deep and comfortable. One or two toys lay around on the floor, and Karl automatically picked them up, despite a grimace from his sister-in-law. The sun streamed in through the window and it was unbelievably satisfying to sink into one of the soft-cushioned armchairs and look at that view with the warm sun on her face.

'This view is fabulous!' She looked across at Karl, her pleasure shining brightly in her eyes and turning them almost amber in colour. Fringed around with dark lashes and tipped intriguingly at their corners, they gave her small face a vaguely oriental look. 'I could sit here for ever and look out of this window!'

'You like it here?'

Once more that oddly anxious appeal puzzled her, and she looked at her hostess's flushed and pretty face, and smiled. 'I think it's wonderful! It must be marvellous to actually live with a view like this.'

'Then you will come?'

Too confused to answer, Sophie glanced between Karl and Lisa, then once more Karl took matters into his own capable hands. He sat down beside her, pulling his chair close, so that she felt a curious sense of intimacy about being in that big room with him, as if they were alone amid all that vast snowy whiteness.

'I should have warned you, yes? I should have said something, given you some clue, but I did not——' He spread his big hands and shrugged, laughing shortly. 'I was afraid you would not come with me if you knew what I had in mind, Sophie.'

It was becoming clear to Sophie at last. He had promised to help her break away from Flora's demanding hold, and this must be what he had had in mind. It accounted for Lisa Bruner's anxiety concerning her opinion too, although she suspected that any help Lisa might want would be purely temporary. She obviously brought up her own children, and if the post was to be temporary it did not really solve anything.

'Lisa is to make me an uncle again very soon,' Karl

told her. 'She needs someone to help with Hugo and Hans while she is having the new baby, Sophie, and I suggested you. Anton is often away and it is good that she has someone younger as well as old Hilde, until the time comes. I have promised Anton that I know of a very charming girl who will please both Lisa and the boys—and here you are!'

She was tempted, she was so very tempted, Sophie frankly admitted it, but the thought of Claude's small, solemn little face kept intruding, and she could imagine his look if he learned she was leaving him. She would willingly leave Flora, but Claude was another matter, and she looked at Karl anxiously, wishing she knew better how to put her feelings into words.

'You do not like the idea?' He did not believe it, she knew from his voice, and he would find it hard to understand her attitude when he knew so well how Flora made use of her. 'What is there that you do not like, little one, eh?'

'Oh, nothing, nothing at all—it's a wonderful idea!' That rather childish endearment he used made her uneasily self-conscious with Lisa Bruner sitting there with them, and she held her hands together in her lap. 'It's just that—it's just that I don't like leaving Claude. You know how he is, Karl.' She appealed to him to understand. 'Flora has no time for him and he needs someone to—to fend for him.'

'My dear child!' Karl's big brown hands reached out and enclosed hers with unbelievable gentleness. 'You cannot devote your entire life to Claude. Flora will be marrying again before very long, and when that happens I have no doubt at all that Rudi Dauzan will lose no time in demanding to have his son returned to him. Claude is very fond of his grandmother, is he not?'

Sophie nodded, unable to deny that the Comtesse Dauzan was the kindest woman Claude could wish for as his guardian, and the best possible thing that could happen would be for him to be returned to her care. But something else was occupying Sophie's mind at the moment and momentarily blocking out everything else. Karl sounded so very sure that Flora would be marrying again very soon, and to be sure, he surely must be the man she was going to marry.

Her mind spun chaotically for a second or two, trying to imagine Claude's hurt if his beloved Karl's first thought after marrying his mother was to be rid of him to the care of his grandmother. 'Sophie?' His voice brought her back from speculation, and she looked at him for a moment with searching, puzzled eyes.

'Yes, of course,' she said in a small voice. 'He's very fond of the Comtesse.'

'Then you will come, will you not, Sophie?'

Lisa Bruner's softly anxious voice made itself heard, and there was nothing Sophie could do but smile at her. She looked again at the impressiveness of the snowy peaks and the vast panorama of mountains scattered with dark pines and little houses like dolls' houses. It would be a wonderful place to live, even for a short time, and if Karl came to visit his sister-in-law—She dismissed that train of thought hastily when she remembered his certainty that Flora would marry again very soon.

Turning back to Lisa Bruner, she started to say something, but before she could utter a word, the door of the room burst open and the three little boys came running in, their faces flushed with excitement and all talking at once in mingled English, French and German.

Laughing at the resultant babel, Karl held up his hands. 'One only,' he begged. 'One only, please! Hugo, you are eldest, you tell us what it is that you find so exciting.'

'An avalanche!' Hugo announced with obvious relish, and turned to his brother and Claude and laughed. 'No one will be able to leave until it is cleared —that is good, eh?'

CHAPTER FOUR

HOWEVER excited the boys were at the idea of being isolated by a blocked road, Sophie's reaction was less enthusiastic, for she could foresee any number of difficulties. She would have to let Flora know where they were as soon as possible, but it was not something she looked forward to at all. Karl apparently having turned down the opportunity of driving her to Schatzheim, Flora was not going to take a very lenient view of his taking Sophie with him to see his family; the fact of their possibly being stranded there would be the last straw.

News of the avalanche would have reached Brunnenheim by now, but so far Flóra had no idea that her son was involved. Someone would have to telephone her and let her know, and Sophie would much rather it was Karl who did it. They had just finished lunch when she raised the matter and from his expression it was clear that he knew what she had in mind.

'We—I should let Flora know where we are,' Sophie ventured. 'She'll be worried when we don't come back within a reasonable time, and it's likely to take some time to clear the road, isn't it?'

'At least twenty-four hours, according to reports, and I dare say that the estimates are under rather than over, to avoid too much concern.' Karl was smiling as he scooped up another forkful of cherry tart. 'You would rather *I* let Flora know, eh, Sophie?'

She nodded without hesitation. 'Would you? I think it will be better coming from you, and I'll be very grateful, Karl.'

He watched her while he put the cherry tart into his mouth and ate it with obvious enjoyment. Then reaching for his glass he nodded before swallowing the contents. 'Very well, I will do so as soon as we have finished lunch.'

'Thank you.'

A ghost of a smile hovered about his mouth while he watched her, and teased her for her reluctance to speak to Flora herself. 'You are afraid of what she will say to you, yes?' Seeing the hasty glance she gave in Claude's direction, he shook his head firmly and hurried on before she could answer. 'No, no, I shall not tease you, it is not fair of me!'

He need not have concerned himself with Claude's reaction, in fact, for he was far too busy disposing of his own portion of *Kirschtorte* to bother about anything else at the moment. Nothing was further from his mind than the possibility of his mother being concerned about him. He was with people he liked and trusted, and that was all that concerned him.

Sophie had never seen him eat so well, and she thought probably his two young companions made a difference to the size of his appetite. The two Bruner boys ate heartily and Lisa had provided an excellent lunch for them.

Käsesuppe, a delicious cheese soup, was followed by a friccassé of pork and the incredibly rich and delicious cherry tart with whipped cream. The children had fruit juice to drink and the adults an excellent vintage Swiss wine that left a most pleasurable glow in its wake, so that Sophie felt very relaxed and at ease as they came to the end of the meal. Even the thought of breaking the news to Flora had only momentarily troubled her, and now that Karl had undertaken to do that, she could relax again.

Lisa's only help in the house was the elderly Hilde, so Sophie volunteered to help clear away and wash the dishes while Lisa rested, something she had insisted on so firmly that Lisa had eventually given in and left her to help while she sat and talked to Karl. The dishes were washed and Sophie was putting away plates in an elaborately carved pine dresser when Karl came into the kitchen.

He was fastening up his topcoat when he came in, and the sight of her domesticated image in a borrowed apron seemed to amuse him. 'An apron suits you!' His eyes gleamed warmly in his tanned face, taking note of the hasty way she avoided looking at him. 'I am taking the boys to look at the blockade on the road—would you like to come with us, Sophie?'

'To look at the avalanche?' Doubt showed in her eyes and her voice, and she could imagine Flora's horror at the idea of taking such chances. 'Is it safe, Karl?'

She should have known, of course, that he was unlikely to be taking his nephews if there was any likelihood of it being dangerous, but the expression in his eyes made allowances for her anxiety and the reason for it. 'Would I be taking Hugo and Hans if there was any danger to them?'

'No, of course you wouldn't.' She laughed a little unsteadily, trying to make him understand. 'I don't know much about situations like this, so you'll have to forgive me being a bit cautious; especially about taking Claude.'

'Of course, I understand your concern, but there is absolutely no need for you to worry—so will you not come with us?'

'I'd love to!'

In trying to undo the borrowed apron she succeeded in tangling the strings somehow, and she clucked impatiently as she tugged blindly behind her back, struggling with the stubborn knot. Without a word Karl turned her round, pushed her hands away and had the strings undone in a matter of seconds. As he handed her the apron from behind, his laughter riffled through the dark hair on her nape and brushed her skin with its tingling warmth.

'Do not be so impatient, little one, we will not go without you!'

His patience and gentleness were welcome, but not so the suggestion of patronage that Sophie's sensitive ear detected, and she turned and looked at him over her shoulder, dark lashes like silken fringes on her cheeks and concealing her eyes.

'I wish you wouldn't sound quite so much as if you regard me in the same category as the boys, Karl! I'm in charge of Claude and you've suggested I'm capable of caring for your nephews, so I'm not just another child!'

Hilde was a little hard of hearing and her English was not very good, but something in Sophie's voice caught her attention and she looked across at her while she continued to put knives and forks into a drawer. It would hardly have been surprising if Karl was angry, but from his voice he wasn't, and she preferred not to look at his face just yet.

'Are you complaining that I treat you like a child, Sophie?'

Uneasily aware of Hilde's presence, Sophie shrugged.

She was already regretting her outburst, but there was little she could do about it now, except try to make him understand what had prompted it. 'You probably don't even realise it,' she ventured with a tentative smile as she turned to face him again. 'I suppose it has to do with the fact that you knew me when I was much younger.'

'Three years?' He smiled and something about it aroused curious responses in her. 'That is not so long, Sophie—not to me. You are very much the same girl you were then, except that you are now even prettier.' His voice softened and a long hand reached out to lightly touch her cheek. 'And much too much sadder.'

Once again Sophie's senses rebelled against being in a situation which three years ago would have thrilled her. Then Karl had been the centre of her existence; now his opinion was of less importance to her, and he had no right to speak as he was when he had all but told her that he was going to marry Flora.

She shook her head to deny the part of her that still responded to him. 'I'm probably more serious, though I don't think I'm sad,' she told him, 'but I'm certainly different from what I was three years ago, Karl, I can assure you. I've grown up and I see things very differently.'

'And people also?' Karl suggested softly, then smiled at the swift colour in her cheeks, just as aware of Hilde's interest. His attention caught by shrill voices in the hall, he glanced over his shoulder and pulled a face. 'The boys grow impatient, Sophie—will you still come with us?'

'I'll get my jacket.'

Her exit was blocked by the three boys suddenly bursting into the kitchen, all talking at once, and she turned to watch as they surrounded Karl. He shushed them with a mock fierceness that deceived no one, and she was smiling to herself as she went to collect her coat—Karl had an unfailing way with children as well as with women.

Lisa had her jacket ready for her, and she smiled a little absently at the noise coming from the kitchen. Her attitude seemed to suggest that she had quite the wrong idea about Sophie's relationship with Karl, and to Sophie that was a little puzzling. She found it difficult to believe that Lisa did not know about Karl's plans with regard to Flora, and she must surely realise that he looked upon Sophie simply as someone he had known years ago and had in all probability forgotten about in the years between.

As she took her jacket from her Sophie noticed her catch her breath and close her eyes for a moment, and she looked at her anxiously. 'Are you all right, Mrs Bruner?'

Lisa shook her head firmly, smiling again. 'I am quite all right, Sophie, just what you call a twinge, *hein*?' She laughed to dismiss any suggestion of something more serious and pulled a face. 'And you will please to call me Lisa. It is much more friendly, is it not?'

'Yes, of course, I'd like to, Lisa.' Sophie regarded the pretty and slightly pale face seriously. 'But are you sure we should leave you?'

'But of course!' Lisa waved away any suggestion that she was not perfectly fit. 'If something should happen I do not think you or Karl would make the very good *Hebamme*—the midwife—eh?' She laughed lightly enough and she looked a little less pale now, Sophie had to admit. 'Also I have Hilde,' Lisa went on, still set on reassuring her. 'She is used to babies and she will get the doctor if he is needed, so there is nothing for you to worry about, yes?'

'If you say so.'

'I do say so.' A gentle hand squeezed her arm and she smiled once more. 'But I am glad that you are here to be with us, Sophie. Now, you go with Karl and the boys, eh?'

Almost reassured, Sophie nodded. 'I'd better hurry too—they sound very impatient, though Karl seems to cope with them easily enough.'

'So!' Lisa agreed with a faintly suggestive smile. 'He will make a very good father, I think.'

It was a matter that made her curiously uneasy when she thought of Flora being the mother of his children, and Sophie merely nodded without committing herself to an opinion, starting visibly when a hand reached round from behind her and took her jacket from her unresisting fingers.

'Come,' Karl said, and held her coat while she put it on. 'You take so long, little one, we thought you had forgotten us!' Turning to his sister-in-law while Sophie buttoned her coat, he apparently noticed nothing amiss with her, and he bent to plant a light kiss on her cheek. 'You will be O.K., *Liebchen*?'

'I will be O.K.,' Lisa returned his smile mischievously. 'You take care of Sophie and the boys, eh?'

His hands on her shoulders brought Sophie an awareness of his strength when his fingers curved for a moment and impressed her flesh even through the thickness of her jacket. Then a hand slid under her arm.

'We shall not be very long, and I will see to it that nothing happens to any of the children.' His hand pressed briefly once more into her arm, reminding her of her earlier objection, and she glanced up in time to catch a bright challenging smile in his eyes. 'Shall we go now, Sophie?'

It gave Sophie a curious sense of isolation, she found, to see the road they had travelled only a short time ago completely blocked by snow. They viewed it from a distance, but even so the great white barrier was awe-inspiring, sweeping on down into the valley and bowing the tops of the trees below them in its path.

The ski-runs were for the most part deserted for the moment, while safety checks were made, and there was a feeling of pregnant stillness about, as if the whole snowy vastness waited for something else to happen. Above the village the barrier of trees looked so fragile against the enormous weight of snow and it sometimes happened, as in this instance, that the barrier was not sufficient to restrain it.

When that happened it rolled on down, uprooting some trees in its descent and tipped over into the valley, glistening like powdered crystal until it found its level. For all its menace, Sophie found it incredibly beautiful and she ventured the opinion without quite knowing what to expect from Karl by way of a reaction.

He looked up at the broken trees, no less flimsy than those that guarded the village, and a hint of a smile hovered about his mouth. 'I suppose it is,' he allowed. 'No one was hurt in this instance, for which we must be thankful, but avalanches are not always so benign, Sophie; they can be killers.'

He was still watching the heights above Schläfing itself, and it occurred to Sophie that he had come out here with the object of judging the likelihood of further falls as much as to see what had already fallen. It gave her a sudden feeling of coldness in her stomach that made her shiver, and she placed a hand on his arm as she looked up at him.

'Karl.'

His face was serious when he turned, but seeing her expression he smiled and strong fingers closed around hers, bringing warmth and reassurance. 'I do not think there will be any more falls,' he told her. 'I am not an expert, of course, but there are signs that appear before-hand sometimes and——' He shrugged his broad shoulders and squeezed her hand once more. 'We must wait and see how long we must stay here—I do not think we should expect to leave before two days.'

'Two days!' Already in her mind's eye Sophie could see Flora's angry face when she learned that Karl was likely to be stranded for two days in Sophie's company. 'Does Flora—did you tell Flora how long it could be?'

He pulled a wry face, but there was laughter in his eyes and in the curve of his mouth. Whatever Flora's reaction had been to the news, it had obviously not disturbed him overmuch. 'Flora was not in the best mood to receive the news that we are stranded up here,' he told her. 'I had forgotten when I telephoned that she might not be back from Schatzheim with Robert St John, but she was.'

Sophie had forgotten too, and she looked at him curiously, for something must surely have gone wrong if Flora and Robert were already back. 'She was back?'

'Just as I rang her.' He glanced at her from the corner of his eye, speculating on her reaction, she realised. 'It seems that Robert St John did not make a very—satis-factory escort for the lady—they did not even stay for lunch.'

'Oh dear, poor Robert!'

Her sympathy was apparently unexpected, for he cocked an eyebrow at her in query. 'You are sorry for him?'

It was perhaps not the most tactful thing to say to him in the circumstances, but on occasion Sophie was apt to speak without first choosing her words. 'He's got a—a thing about Flora,' she explained. 'He thinks she's the most wonderful creature on earth at the moment and he'll be shattered if she's quarrelled with him.'

'Ah, I see!' He tucked her arm firmly under his while they stood on the snowbound road watching the children. 'You do not mind that he is captivated?'

'Not in the least,' Sophie assured him, wondering what on earth he was leading up to. 'I've only known the man a couple of days.'

'Ah!' That evidently satisfied him on some point, and he put his free hand over hers and squeezed. 'I think it is as well that you have agreed to come to Lisa, little one.'

A hasty glance revealed no significant change in his expression, but he had something further to tell her about his call to Flora, she felt sure, and she had an uneasy idea what it might be. 'Was Flora furious about me bringing Claude here?'

'Yes, she was.' He made no attempt to sugar the pill, and Sophie was undecided whether or not she was glad about it. 'Flora no longer wishes to have you in her employ. I explained that the fault, if it was a fault, was more mine than yours, but she was so full of her anger that she would not listen to reason.' He turned and looked down at her, his darkly tanned face given a curious luminosity by the sun-bright snow. 'But you expected such a reaction from her, did you not, Sophie?'

There was little point in denying it, or in making a fuss, especially now she had made up her mind to take the job with Lisa, and she nodded. Karl would know as well as she did that Flora was as angry about his being with Sophie as she was concerned for her son.

'Yes, I expected something like that,' she agreed.

'But it need not worry you so much now that you have decided to stay here with Lisa, eh?' He looked across to where Claude was playing happily with Hugo and Hans, as yet unaware of the changes that had already been made in his life. 'You will miss Claude, I think, as he will miss you.'

'He's lonely for other children.' Sophie watched Claude for a moment, her heart once more rebelling at the thought of deserting him when he had come so to depend on her. 'If only Flora had——' She shrugged, remembering that he had told her Rudi Dauzan was likely to claim back his son when Flora remarried. 'I suppose he'll be happy enough with his grandmother, he's always liked the Comtesse Dauzan.'

Strong fingers squeezed hers gently and reassuringly. 'Maybe Flora will have other children when she remarries. It will be good for Claude to have brothers to share his play as Hugo and Hans do, do you not agree?'

And Flora would have other children with Karl, Sophie thought; he would want children of his own. But the idea of discussing it with him she rejected fiercely, and snatched her hand free of his firm clasp as she shook her head. 'That's something you'd better talk to Flora about,' she said. 'I don't think she'd take kindly to the idea of you discussing it with me!'

'Sophie?'

She ignored his obvious perplexity and called Claude

over. 'Let's go, shall we? We can't make it go away any quicker by looking at it!'

They all three came running to join them, eyes gleaming in small bright faces, and it struck Sophie very forcibly that she had seldom seen Claude look happier than he was now, stranded here on the mountain with her and Karl. As far as he was concerned the situation was ideal, and she only wished she could enjoy it as much. It would have been very different three years ago; then she would have thought herself in heaven to be here with Karl. But then there had been no complication like Flora, and Sophie had felt very differently about Karl.

'We will go back now if you wish to.' There was an edge on Karl's voice that reminded her of that night on the Schillenberg, when she had let him know that she did not want to be beholden to him. *'Kommt!'* The fact that he spoke to the boys in German betrayed his mood, and they obeyed without hesitation, though they gave both her and their uncle a curious look before running on to join Claude again.

'Karl . . .'

Sophie hesitated, not sure what to say now that she had his attention. They had to be together in the same house for at least another twenty-four hours and there was no sense in making the situation any worse by being at odds with him. It had been her own doing too, she had to admit that; because she had been too touchy about Flora and him, but it was not easy to put her feelings into words.

As if he sensed her difficulty that glimmer of amusement appeared once more in his eyes and he laughed. 'I forgive you for—biting off my head?—for we must

not quarrel if we are to be sharing the same house for
the next two days or so, eh?'

'I didn't intend to quarrel with you.' His arm was
tucked under hers and a large gloved hand curled about
her slim wrist as they walked. Looking up at him
briefly, she smiled. 'I can be a bit bad-tempered when
I'm nervous,' she warned him. 'You'll have to take that
as my excuse.'

'And you are nervous of staying here with me and
Lisa and the children?'

The towering peaks seemed to loom menacingly as
they neared the house again, and she shivered. It was
safe enough, Karl had promised, and she trusted his
judgment enough to accept that. 'I just feel a bit—awkward, being in an entirely new situation,' she confessed.
'I'll do my best not to let it show.'

'Good!' He added something more in German, very
softly, but she had no idea what it meant, and the lean
hardness of him pressed to her side was comfort enough
at the moment.

It was a fairly long walk back to the house, and the
three boys were there some time ahead of them, racing
along the snow-banked road to see who could gain the
house first. Hugo, having the longest legs, was easily
the winner and he ran on ahead of Hans and Claude,
calling out to them in triumph. It was several minutes
later that he came back to meet Sophie and Karl, still
running but looking much more serious and taking his
uncle's hand as if he needed his support.

He spoke in German, but it was clear from his expression that it was something that concerned him deeply,
and Sophie guessed what it must be. She was about
to ask, but Karl forestalled her. Urging Hugo in her

direction, he hurried off ahead, turning to speak over his shoulder to her as he went.

'I will go on ahead and see what is happening, Sophie. The doctor is with Lisa—she is having her baby too soon!'

It was barely five minutes since Lisa's baby girl was born, and Sophie breathed freely for the first time since Hugo had come back to tell Karl the baby was arriving. The road was impassable so that the prearranged ambulance had been unavailable, but they had managed quite well in their improvised conditions.

The doctor was middle-aged and competent, but Sophie had the feeling that he would far rather have had his patient taken to hospital, though the baby was perfect and Lisa as well as could be expected. It was the first time in her life that Sophie had witnessed the birth of a baby first hand and she had found the experience both alarming and exciting.

The baby was slightly premature and Lisa had not had an easy time, but she was sleeping now and her new baby warmly wrapped, so tiny it seemed incredible she could have caused so much effort to achieve her arrival. Hilde had been the doctor's main ally, but Sophie was convinced that her own part had contributed to the safe arrival too, and she felt strangely elated as she made her way to the big room with the view, to tell Karl that he had a niece.

With the sleeves of her sweater still rolled up above her elbows and wearing one of Lisa's aprons, she opened the door and looked across at Karl where he sat on the edge of a chair supervising some kind of game that was going on on the rug at his feet. It seemed a very long way to where he sat, and she was glad that he got to his feet the minute she came into the room, and came to meet her part way.

'Lisa?'

His anxiety was plain in his eyes, and Sophie smiled to reassure him. 'She's very tired, but she's well and very pleased with herself.'

'And the baby?'

'A little girl—and she's beautiful!' Her eyes brimmed with tears of reaction and she promptly buried her head against Karl's comfortingly substantial shoulder.

His arms came around her quite naturally and without hesitation, pulling her close to him. 'Oh, Sophie!' He was laughing a little unsteadily, with his face buried in the dark softness of her hair and his mouth close beside her ear, whispering words in his own tongue that fluttered warmly against her neck and made her reluctant to lift her head and look at him. 'Why are you crying, little one? Lisa is well, is she not? And the baby is beautiful, you have said so.'

'And I get sentimental about babies!' She was seeking excuses for her tears, although she knew from his expression that Karl understood just how she felt. Taking a handkerchief from his pocket, he gently wiped away the tears, then smiled down at her in a way that made her tremble so much that breaking his hold on her seemed the only solution. 'It's a pretty traumatic experience, you know, assisting at the birth of a baby, however small a part you play; especially when it's the first time!'

'I imagine it is so.'

He obviously found her rejection of him puzzling, but she avoided looking at him again and gave her attention to the boys instead. They were watching

curiously, obviously knowing there was something going on that they did not quite understand, and Hugo,
being the eldest, was their spokesman.

He was the one who looked most like Karl, and it
struck Sophie suddenly that Karl's children would
probably look just as Hugo did—his and Flora's. Shaking her head firmly to dismiss such oddly discomfiting
speculation, she started to say something to Hugo, but
he forestalled her with his question, addressing himself
to his uncle.

'A girl?' he asked in English, picking on the only
detail he was sure of, and Karl nodded.

'You have a sister, that is good, yes?' Hugo's obvious
and undisguised doubt seemed to amuse him and he
laughed, one hand on the boy's head. 'You would have
preferred another brother, I suppose?'

'I like a sister!' Hans spoke up quickly from the
other side of him, as if he feared an exchange might
be made simply on Hugo's say-so, and Karl ruffled his
blond hair affectionately.

'Ah, but you are more gallant, little Hans, eh?' His
glance fell on Claude who was standing a little apart
from the rest of them and looking rather lonely in his
isolation. 'What would your choice be, Claude? A
brother or a sister?'

Scarcely knowing what it was he was being asked
about, since there was no question of his having either
as far as he knew, Claude shrugged in that explicit
French way he had, and shook his head. His isolation
served to remind Sophie that she was soon to part from
him, and she hugged him suddenly and impulsively,
giving Karl a look that defied him to blame her for
feeling guilty about it.

'It's difficult to understand what it's like to have

either when you're an only child,' she told him. 'I know.'

'Yes, of course you do.' The warmth of sympathy in his voice Sophie found almost unbearable, but she could not have him realise how much it affected her and she looked away. 'You must miss your father a great deal.'

'I do.' Claude's small cuddly body was held close in her arms and she looked anywhere but at Karl. 'That's why I don't know——'

'No, Sophie!' He seemed to realise how sharply he had spoken, and his voice softened noticeably when he went on, touching her senses with his gentleness. 'It is not possible, little one, it is just not possible now, you know that; and you have been the—the butt of Flora's temper for too long.'

She knew it, Sophie told herself, while she hugged Claude to her, but she did not want to think of Claude looking on her as having deserted him. 'I know.' Her voice was husky and not much more than a whisper, and she could not hold Claude any longer, he was restless to be away from her and joining in with his new friends again.

She stood up, feeling oddly lonely herself suddenly, although without reason, for she had a place here with Lisa and the boys, at least until Lisa was well enough to manage without her again. After that—well, that was something that would have to be thought out when the time came. Maybe Karl would find her someone else in the same situation.

'I will go and see the doctor and then ring Anton with the news.' He waited until she looked at him again, then smiled, and his brown face was etched with tiny lines at the corners of his eyes. 'Thank you for your help, Sophie; I do not remember saying it when you came in.'

Remembering what *had* happened when she came in, Sophie hastily avoided looking at him. 'It was a pleasure,' she said, and was somewhat surprised to realise how true it was.

The children were all in bed, sleeping soundly after a rather hectic day of excitement. Claude was accommodated in the same room with Hugo and Hans, and the novelty of sharing delighted him so much that there had been a great deal of chattering before they eventually went to sleep. For Sophie too, the evening was very different from the kind she was used to.

Old Hilde had gone to bed early, but Sophie felt far from sleepy and she and Karl sat in the big sitting-room for some time after Hilde bade them goodnight, looking out at the moonlit panorama of mountains and snow, saying little but sharing something that was more than words.

Everything out there seemed to be turned to silver. The moon was full and the air so clear that it appeared to sit right on the tops of the peaks. Down below, only visible if one got up and stood to the window glass, were several small houses, huddled in a valley that seemed ten times its normal size in the moonlight. Tiny yellow dots marked lighted windows, streaking out on to snow that was shadowed by the peaks, like glimmers of warmth in the icy vastness.

'Are you not very tired?' Carl spoke in the semi-darkness, for artificial light would have spoiled the moonlit view. 'You have had a very busy day, Sophie.'

'I've had a very exciting day!'

She was tired but quite unexpectedly excited too,

and she had no inclination to go to bed yet. It had occurred to her that a walk might make her sleepy, but she had dismissed it as impractical, partly because the environment was strange to her and it was night-time.

There was a clearly defined road above the barrier of snow, but she was on strange ground and not inclined to take the chance of falling on the steep, snow-banked incline. Also the cold air was far more likely to make her even more wakeful rather than induce sleep.

She turned her head for a moment and looked at Karl, relaxed and comfortable in another armchair next to hers. 'I'm so comfortable, I hate to move.'

In the shadows of the moonlit room his tanned face had an even stronger appearance than usual, and his blond hair seemed more thick and golden. There was a shiveringly disturbing aura of virile masculinity about him that she found infinitely affecting, though she was trying hard not to let it affect her. His long body was stretched out in the armchair, lazily responsive to the warm room and the air of relaxation, his eyes half-closed, even when he turned his head to smile, teasing her for the very laziness he had succumbed to himself.

'Not even to go for a walk with me?' he asked, and Sophie's heart gave a sudden lurch at the idea of walking in the moonlight with him.

She would not admit to anything like the old feeling for him, but he was a very attractive companion and she had been thinking along the same lines herself. There was no reason why her senses should be responding to him the way they were, but possibly the moonlight had something to do with that. The cold night air would bring her sharply back to earth.

'I'd like that!' She remembered something suddenly,

and looked up at him as he got to his feet, reacting swiftly as always. 'I have to get back in time to see to the baby's feed, though. With premature babies, they have to be fed more often.'

'Yes, of course, but there is plenty of time yet.' His big hands reached down invitingly and she put her own into them, almost wincing when his strong hard fingers closed over hers and he pulled her to her feet. Sometimes she wondered if he realised just how strong he was, and how bruisingly hard his grip could be. 'Hilde will hear if Lisa calls, but she will trust you to bring the little one to her when it is time.'

'The little one!' She looked up at him and pulled a face. 'She shares the title too, I see. Doesn't she have a name yet?'

She had spent far more time with Lisa since the baby was born than Karl had, but each time she had asked about a name she thought Lisa evaded an answer, and she had supposed the matter of a name for a girl had not been decided. Karl was smiling and holding her hand as they walked across the room.

'Lisa wishes to call her Sophie Carla, and I think Anton will agree—he is so grateful that we were here when the baby was born.'

'Sophie?' A thrill of pleasure brought a smile to her eyes and she made no attempt to conceal her delight in the idea. 'Oh, but that's wonderful! I can understand Lisa wanting to call her Carla, but—well, I'm a stranger!'

They walked out into the hall and he found her jacket for her, holding it while she pushed her arms into the sleeves, keeping his voice low because the house was asleep except for the two of them. 'You will not be a stranger for very long, Sophie, eh?' A hand brushed across the back of her neck, moving her hair aside as she settled the collar of her coat, and she caught her breath on the shivering gentleness of its touch. When she turned he was already in his own jacket and fastening the collar under his chin, and he smiled as he took her arm. 'Now, let us sneak out into the night, little one, like—like lovers, *hein?*' He laughed and ran a light finger-tip down her flushed cheek. 'Forgive me, Sophie, the moonlight makes me a little lightheaded!'

Outside it was cold; bitterly, bitingly cold, but as clear as crystal and smelling of pine from the shattered trees that stood upended and piercing the fallen snow that swept down into the valley. It was still too, although a breath of wind stirred the powdery surface into occasional little puffs like dust about their feet; and it was quiet as only mountains can be.

There was a low light burning still in Lisa's room that reminded Sophie she must be back in time to attend to her new charge, and she kept it firmly in mind as she walked beside Karl down the steep hill. It was better to keep something in mind instead of letting herself become too conscious of the arm that was entwined with hers, and the fingers curled about her wrist.

Without the boys they went a little nearer to the snow barrier, but still stayed at a safe distance, and for a while they stood looking down, with the village behind them and the way down to Brunnenheim closed fast against them. It gave her a flutter of panic suddenly to realise how completely they were cut off, and she shivered involuntarily.

The hand on her arm tightened its hold and Karl smiled down at her curiously. 'Are you too cold?'

'No, not at all!' She laughed a little uncertainly,

preferring not to confess her fears at the moment. 'I just—shivered, that's all. Nothing significant.'

Evidently satisfied, Karl looked around him, then down into the silent valley again, and his voice sounded curiously absent, more as if he was speaking to himself rather than to her. 'It is a strange sensation up here in the mountains, quite unlike anything else. It gives one a sense of being *göttlich.*' He became aware of Sophie's puzzled frown, and smiled. 'Divine,' he explained. 'Like a god, yes?'

It so closely followed her own thoughts as they drove up there that Sophie nodded without hesitation and unconsciously hugged more closely to him, with her eyes on the moonlit valley. 'Godlike.' She laughed a little uncertainly and nodded. 'Yes, I know what you mean, Karl.'

She did not notice him actually turn, but he was facing her, she realised suddenly, and looking down into her face with an intensity that stirred unbidden responses in her and at the same time rang a warning bell in her brain. His mouth had a sensual strength that her eyes found fascinating and could not look away from, and the hands on her arms were irresistible as they drew her closer to the vigorous leanness of him until his arms enfolded her firmly.

'Karl!' The whispered plea was as much a warning to him as a reminder to herself, but it went unheeded.

Karl said nothing, but the darkly tanned face with its light, bright blue eyes came breathtakingly close until the warmth of his mouth was on hers, lightly brushing her lips until she closed her eyes against the temptation of it. Then he kissed her with such fervour that she felt she must have stopped breathing altogether, and she made no more pretence at resistance.

Her hands spread wide over the soft suede jacket he wore, and then closed tightly against his broad back when he released her mouth and pressed his lips to her neck and the throbbing softness of her throat, snuggling his face into the warmth of the fur collar of her jacket. It was only when she opened her eyes and saw the gleaming brightness of his hair that she remembered Flora.

Turning her face away from him, she beat at his chest with both hands in mounting anger for her own weakness, heedless of how hard she hit him, only anxious that he should let her go. She should have thought about Flora. Her only excuse was that she had been caught unawares; but Karl's action had been deliberate, and he should have been more conscious of how wrong it was in the circumstances.

Slipping away from the hands that only reluctantly let her go, she turned back towards the house, her breath billowing from parted lips in small clouds, one after the other with the rapidity of her breathing. She hated herself for weakening and at the moment she hated Karl for making her weaken. Those youthful dreams she had once cherished so earnestly were a thing of the past and she had meant them to stay that way; she *still* meant them to stay that way.

'Sophie!'

He was coming after her and she knew there was no chance of avoiding him, for there was nowhere else for her to go except back to the house. Her heart thudding wildly, she walked quickly up the steep road, her breathing short and urgent, and caught in her throat suddenly when a hand on her arm spun her round to face him, and she looked into a face whose expression was hard to read in the chill of the moonlight.

She was panting from her exertions, and even Karl showed some sign of breathlessness, but he held her arm in a grip that was much too hard for her to break, and tight enough to make her wince when she tried. 'Sophie, wait!' He pulled her round again when she tried to turn from him, and she could almost feel the intensity of the blue eyes as they watched her for a second before he went on. 'Why do you always put up this—barrier against me?'

Those softened 'W's made his accent seem so much stronger, and Sophie shook her head against the effect of it. Her cheeks were flushed and she did not look at him, but tried again to free her arm from that inescapable grip. 'I have to get back, Karl, you know that.'

'No, you do not—not yet!' She simply shook her head and would probably have gone on standing there in silence, but he quite suddenly gave a great sigh and the hand on her arm eased enough for her to have evaded it had she tried. 'I do not know where I go so wrong with you, Sophie, that you reject me so determinedly.' He laughed, a short hard and humourless sound. 'I am not usually so clumsy, but with you I always do the wrong thing, do I not, little one?' A bitter twist of a smile distorted his mouth and he shrugged. 'It is a fact I am reluctant to face, but you seem to dislike being in my arms!'

Sophie had never felt so incredibly unsure of herself in her life before. He must realise why she had brought that last stunning episode to a hasty close, surely; how could he not? And yet he was smiling at her in a wry and slightly apologetic way that would have been irresistible if she had not been firm with herself. They were within sight of the house, and the light in Lisa's window beckoned like a beacon against the snowy background. Following the direction of her gaze, Karl nodded his head.

'Very well, little Sophie, I will not keep you from your duties, but one day——' He laughed as he tucked her arm firmly under his and pressed it to the warmth of his body, and Sophie prayed that the road would be open and the way clear before that day arrived.

CHAPTER FIVE

THERE was a great deal of activity on the blocked road all the following day, and by evening it was thought that the way would be passable by the next morning. Sophie heard the news with mixed feelings, for despite the threat of further falls and the isolation they had endured the past couple of days, there had been a comforting sense of closeness that she had enjoyed.

Now that their way was clear she anticipated going back with Karl to hand Claude back to his mother and to pick up her things from the hotel room, and the thought of facing Flora again became less attractive every minute. Nor had she told Claude yet about her changing position, and that more than anything troubled her when she thought of how hurt he was likely to be.

The fact that she had been kept busy since the baby was born was all to the good, for while she was so occupied with helping Hilde her mind as well as her hands were occupied. There were extra feeds involved as well as an enormous amount of washing, so that she had very little time in which to contemplate her own situation. It was only when she looked at Claude, playing happily with Hugo and Hans, that she felt the pressing need to take some decisive step.

It had occurred to her that by now Flora might have reconsidered her hasty dismissal, and she was intelligent enough to realise the difficulty in replacing Sophie with someone who was prepared to do as much for the meagre salary she paid. Flora might well be hoping that when Lisa no longer had need of her services, Sophie would ask to have her old job back, and that would once more give her the upper hand.

As far as telling Claude was concerned, Sophie secretly had hopes that Karl might take it on himself to break the news. He had come to her aid several times lately, in fact it was rather discomfiting to realise just how she had come to rely on him in various ways lately.

At the moment Lisa was sleeping, and Sophie was settling the baby back into her cradle when a tap on the bedroom door made her glance anxiously at Lisa to see that she had not been woken. Tucking her tiny namesake in warmly, she hurried over to see who it was, hoping to forestall another knock.

Finger to her lips, she stepped out on to the landing and found Karl waiting there. 'Lisa and Sophie are asleep,' she whispered, and he nodded, a hand under her arm as they made their way downstairs.

Obviously he had been outdoors, probably to check on the progress of the road clearing, for he had the raw smell of cold air about him, and his tanned face glowed with exertion. Once out of earshot in the hall, he wasted no time, but came straight to the point.

'The road is almost clear, another hour or two at most, and I have told Claude that I shall be driving him back to Brunnenheim as soon as it is open, Sophie.'

She looked up quickly, startled to realise that things had been brought to a head without her even being aware of it. Karl held the door of the sitting-room open and ushered her in before him, closing it again on the sound of children's voices coming from the playroom across the hall.

It had been done. The task she had been putting off for so long because she did not have the necessary nerve to face it had been accomplished almost without effort, it seemed, and for a moment she resented his doing it without consulting her. Then reason prevailed, and she heaved an inward sigh.

'So you've told him?'

She stood facing him, realising that he was watching her in a curiously speculative way that made her uneasy. There were too many distractions running around in her brain for her to concentrate as she should on the matter in hand. For one thing the thought of Karl returning to Flora while she stayed on there with his sister-in-law was something she found herself disliking intensely, though she quickly shook off the sensation. It was Claude she was going to miss, not Karl.

'Did you not wish me to be the one to tell him, Sophie?' Why did he always have to follow her train of thought so accurately? It was disturbing as well as annoying, and that hint of a smile he teased her with, seemed to suggest he knew that too. 'I thought you would rather I broke the news.'

Like a magnet, that incredible panorama outside drew her to the window and she stood for a moment with her back to him, looking out at the snow and the sunshine shimmering on the peaks. The laughter and voices from the playroom scarcely suggested that anyone in there was troubled about anything, and the thought of Claude taking it in his stride gave her a moment of regret.

'I wanted you to be the one to tell him, Karl, thank you.' She kept her eyes on the scene outside and laughed a little unsteadily. 'I didn't have the nerve.'

'You were afraid he would become upset?'

She had expected Claude to be at least a little upset, and she could not bring herself to face the fact that he wasn't—not yet. But the laughter in the playroom showed how wrong she had been. 'I thought he might have been a *bit* upset about my leaving him.'

'Sophie!' Strong hands on her upper arms pressed into her flesh reassuringly, and his voice stirred the hair on her neck with its warmth. 'I persuaded him that you should stay here to take care of Lisa and the new baby, and he was convinced.' He turned her round to face him and looked down into her face, trying to hold her elusive gaze. 'Will it make you jealous, Sophie, if I say that it is because he is coming back with me that he is less concerned about leaving you?' He laughed and shook his head slowly. 'That sounds very conceited, yes?'

'It sounds very much like the truth.'

She admitted it frankly, but it gave her a strange sense of loss as she stood there, knowing that she had now only to take her leave of Claude, and it would all be over. In many ways she had been quite happy with Flora and Claude, and with Flora there had been a kind of security as long as she kept on the right side of her. Now she had not only to think of an entirely new life, but what came next, when Lisa no longer needed her.

'Well, it seems you've taken care of everything, doesn't it?' Her laugh was tremblingly unsteady and she shook her head. 'At least I haven't to see Flora and explain; I don't think I'd have had the nerve for that either!'

'Sophie?' Long fingers, gently insistent, turned her face to him and she felt a swift flutter of sensation at the light firm touch on her skin. 'You are not regretting this change, are you?'

'A little.' She looked up at him appealingly, hoping he would understand. 'I can't help it, Karl, I've got so—so used to the way things were, but you don't have to worry.'

'You are not going to change your mind about staying with Lisa and the boys?'

'Oh no, of course I won't!' She smiled at him, wondering if he quite realised how impossible it was for her to change her mind. 'I can't very well, can I? Not now Flora's given me the sack.'

'Flora will have realised her mistake by now, and she is probably hoping that you——' He was watching her closely, almost suspiciously, and he kept her face upturned, with his gaze fixed on the quivering softness of her mouth. 'If I thought for one moment that you were thinking of going to Flora and being—humble, I would take you out and smother you in the nearest snowdrift, Sophie!'

The threat was jokingly made, but an underlying seriousness threaded his voice and made her realise that something of the sort had entered her mind, however briefly. Looking up at him, she put a hand over the strong fingers that supported her chin and tried to shake her head.

'You haven't much faith in me, have you, Karl? Don't you trust me?'

'I am not sure!'

His frankness brought a swift flush of colour to her cheeks and she stepped back quickly, knocking his hand from her chin and facing him with bright, indignant eyes. 'In that case maybe you'd better find someone else to look after Lisa and the boys, while I go back and eat humble pie as you seem to expect me to!'

'*Oh* no, Sophie!' His hand settled on her neck, curved to the shape of her head, and there was something about the way he smiled that made her turn from him to gaze out of the window once more. 'You will *not* go back and eat humble pie!'

'Because you say so?' It gave her a strange sense of exhilaration to challenge him, that was quite new to her, and she was aware of him standing almost immediately behind her, close enough for the warmth of his body to touch her whenever he breathed.

'If you like!' A long finger stroked across her neck and brushed her hair aside while he bent and pressed his lips to a spot just below her left ear. 'You will stay here because you have promised me you will do so, and you will not even think of going back to Flora!'

Half turned towards him, she spoke over her shoulder in a low and huskily breathless voice that she scarcely recognised as hers. 'Karl, you really have——'

'No right to expect you to do as you have promised? Oh, but I think I have, little one, and you will not let me down, eh?'

'Haven't I told you I won't? But'—she turned round slowly, her brows drawn—'what happens when Lisa doesn't need me any more, Karl? I might be glad to go back to Flora then. She knows I'm untrained and she makes allowances.'

'She also takes advantage!'

'Oh, I'm so—so *use*less!' It was true, and she faced the fact with a hitherto unrealised sense of frustration. 'If only I was trained for something! Something useful that would help me to earn a living!'

'But you are skilled in caring for children, Sophie.

That is your talent, and Lisa as well as Flora recog-
nises it. You are *quite* capable of earning your living,
little one.'

She should have known that Karl would have the
answer, of course, and he was right in a way. But so far
both situations had been gained through influence
rather than merit, and that was much less satisfying.
Her lack of skills had never troubled her before as it
did now, but it had never before been quite so important.

'I've been lucky so far. Flora needed me to look after
Claude and you felt sorry for me. Yes, you did!' She
looked up at him, a defensive challenge in her eyes.
'You know you'd never have thought about someone
as—as inexperienced as I am if you hadn't wanted to
do something to help me get away from Flora.'

'Oh, you feel so sorry for yourself, hmm?' His
laughter teased her and she felt oddly elated suddenly,
instead of angry. Bending over her, he touched his lips
to hers and laughed again as he put a long forefinger to
the fullness of her lower lip and followed its line. 'Well,
stop being sorry for yourself, because you have no
reason to be! If I had not thought you capable of taking care of Hans and Hugo I would not for a moment
have considered recommending you, no matter if I felt
sorry for you or not, is that quite clear?' She nodded,
and Karl kissed her lightly beside her mouth. 'Lisa
needs you and so do the boys!'

'And when Lisa doesn't need me any more? Are you
going to be my agent, Karl? Or do I—put myself up
for auction?'

He laughed and a long finger traced the line of her
neck as far as the collar of her sweater, then smoothed
upwards again to her cheek. His mouth was pressed

firmly to hers for a moment, then he looked down at her with that gleaming look of laughter in his eyes again.

'We will wait and see what will happen, little one, eh?'

Claude was rather less willing to go without Sophie when it came to the point, but once again Karl persuaded him, by insisting that Lisa and the new baby needed her more than he did, and he eventually went off quite happily, less upset at the parting than Sophie was, and waving from the front passenger seat to his new friends.

As soon as he caught sight of the skiers on the slopes, Sophie thought as she watched him go, everything else would be forgotten. Maybe tonight when he was put to bed, he would miss her, and perhaps even cry for her, and as she watched the car disappear round the bend in the road, she felt a lump in her throat.

The task of coping with two little boys instead of one was not so very different, and she had had the advantage during the last couple of days of having three of them, so that Hans and Hugo were fairly used to her. They seemed somewhat subdued for a while after their uncle was gone, but they were quite amenable to being put to bed when they were told. It was natural that they should be a little confused by events, but she foresaw few difficulties if they behaved as they had so far. Perhaps Karl was right, and she had a natural flair for dealing with children—she liked to think it was true.

A call from Brunnenheim told them that Karl and his passenger had arrived back safely, but Karl had said nothing on the phone about Flora's reaction, and she did not like to ask. His main concern was for his sister-in-law and his nephews. He would be driving up to

Schläfing in a day or two to check on them all, he said,
and Sophie hastily stifled her surprise at his almost
paternal concern for them all. She had learned a great
deal about the man who was the real Karl Bruner
during the past few days.

Much more surprising was the arrival, soon after
lunch the following day, of Robert St John driving a
hired car, and with Flora as his passenger, and Sophie
received them with mixed feelings. 'We've brought your
things.' Robert was unloading her things from the car
and looking at her in a way that suggested he was not
too certain of the kind of welcome they would get.
'Flora thought you'd be needing them, Sophie.'

'Yes, thank you, it is a bit awkward, though Lisa's
lent me some of her things for the time being.'

When she had asked Karl about the transfer of her
luggage, he had promised to see about it for her, but
almost inevitably he would consult Flora, and that
precluded any likelihood of his being allowed to bring
it to her. Flora would put herself to any trouble, rather
than let Karl do some personal service for Sophie. A
glance at Flora was enough to convince anyone that
consideration for Sophie's needs was not the reason for
the visit, but she was too glad to have the rest of her
things to bother about it at the moment, and she invited them both in for a talk.

Whatever malice Flora had in mind she managed to
conceal very well as long as Hilde and the boys were
present. But it must have been galling for her, Sophie
guessed, to think of her isolated up there with Karl
and his family, when she had been unable to persuade
him to drive her to Schatzheim, and Flora did not
easily forgive or forget.

She knew how to bide her time too, and she was very

polite and smiling to Hilde, cooing over the thought of a new baby, though Sophie knew perfectly well that she had no time for children whatever age they were. She put herself out to be very sweet to Hans and Hugo too, but they quite obviously regarded her with suspicion, even though they were very formally polite.

But the strain told, and when Hilde and the boys were out of earshot at last, and Sophie was seeing the visitors out, she made her feelings plain and unmistakable. Narrow-eyed and no longer under any kind of restraint, she turned on Sophie.

'I suppose you thought you were very clever, didn't you?' Her bright blue eyes had the cold glitter of ice, and she showed small even teeth between very red lips as she spoke. 'You surely didn't think I'd go on employing you after you went jaunting off with Karl like that, did you?'

'I didn't go jaunting off, as you call it, Flora. As far as I knew we were simply going for a drive and having lunch somewhere.'

'And you hadn't any idea where, of course?' Sophie had time only to shake her head. There was no point in denying it anyway, for Flora wasn't going to believe anything she said. 'You didn't even tell me you were sneaking off to look for another job! After I'd taken you in when you hadn't a penny to your name, too!'

'And I was grateful, Flora.' She did not say it, but Sophie felt she had paid for whatever charity had prompted the gesture, a hundred times over in the last six mouths. And it was dawning on her gradually that she no longer needed to stay in Flora's good graces to keep her job; the sense of exhilaration that gave her was beyond belief.

'Grateful!'

While Flora blazed at her scornfully, Sophie realised that Robert was looking rather anxious. She felt rather sorry for him, though heaven knew why, for he had let himself be led by the nose into a situation he could no longer control, and impatience tempered her natural sympathy.

'Whatever you believe, Flora, I *was* grateful, but as it happens things worked out for the best. I was going to give you notice when we got back, but first the avalanche and then Lisa's baby arriving prematurely—they were things that Karl and I simply hadn't foreseen.'

'Karl and you!'

Sophie realised, too late, just how that must sound to Flora, but there was nothing she could do to recall it now. Maybe Flora had the right to be angry about it when—— Once more her brain rejected the thought of the wedding Karl had hinted at, and she hurried on with an explanation.

'It was Karl's idea that we came here, Flora.' She had no qualms about putting the onus on to him because he had already done so himself, according to what he had told her the night he telephoned Flora with the news. 'He brought me to see Lisa because she wanted someone to look after her boys, and he knew—well, he knew I wanted to leave you.'

'He knew because you went snivelling to him about how badly you were treated, I suppose!' She was shivering with anger and yet somehow she still managed to keep her voice under control so far, and Sophie vaguely wondered how much longer she could do it. 'You ungrateful, toadying little——'

'Flora, please don't say any more!'

'Oh, shut up!'

Flora turned on Robert with as much fury as she had on Sophie, and Sophie noticed him flinch as if she had struck him a physical blow. 'Don't say things you'll regret, Flora, you know you don't mean them.'

'You're partly to blame for what happened!' She ignored the appeal and curled her lip in a way that left her opinion of him in no doubt. 'If you hadn't been so ready to drive me anywhere you want to go, darling, I'd have been around when Karl got entangled with this scheming little bitch!'

It was unfair to blame him for doing as she wanted, and cruel to mock his rather ingratiating manner towards her, but somehow Sophie felt he had brought it on himself. He did not seem to realise yet that a good deal of Karl's appeal, where Flora was concerned, was the fact that he did not care at all what she wanted, he simply went his own way.

But Robert too had his limits, it seemed, and Sophie noticed the colour in his face suddenly, and a gleam in his eyes that had not been there before. For the past eight days he had followed Flora slavishly, ready to do anything she asked, take her where she wanted to go, just as long as he could be with her.

But he was an intelligent man, and sooner or later his mind was bound to rebel against her treatment of him, and Sophie guessed the moment was now. He had reached his limit and whether or not he would recant later, at the moment he was firmly resolved to make his protest.

'I think you've said quite enough, Flora. If I'd realised that your only reason for coming up here was to quarrel with Sophie, I'd never have brought you!' His voice was stronger and harder than either Sophie or Flora had heard it before, and it was debatable which of them was most surprised. 'Unless you go and get into the car and drive back with me, you can find your own way back to Brunnenheim,' he threatened. 'I'm leaving right now!'

Flora stared at him in stunned disbelief for a moment, scarcely crediting that anyone could speak to her like that, especially anyone she had thought so firmly under her thumb as Robert. Then a dark flush coloured her face, and she clenched her hands tightly over the top of her handbag as she looked at him, brittle and angry.

'Then go!' she told him, in a hard flat voice. 'I'll ring Karl and get him to fetch me!'

It was a vain threat, Sophie suspected, and a glance at Robert showed that he shared the same doubt. So many times Flora had tried to play off Karl against her various admirers, and so often he had refused to co-operate in her schemes. Sophie wondered that she still bothered to try, but Robert, it was quite clear, was fearful as well as confident of the result; for Flora's sake.

Flora turned back to Sophie, her eyes bright and cold as diamonds. 'Where's the telephone?' she demanded.

Stunned for a moment, Sophie merely indicated the telephone that stood in a small alcove nearby, then she flicked another curious glance at Robert. He should have gone, she realised vaguely; by still being there he had already weakened his threat, and Flora knew it. She turned her back on them when Karl answered, and switched on that familiar and slightly sickening voice; softly cooing, hopefully persuasive.

'Karl darling? Look, my sweet, I'm stranded up here at your brother's place, and——' She listened, her smile wavering only slightly. 'I brought Sophie's things for

her. Bobby St John *brought* me, darling, but he's being
nasty.' She pouted, apparently forgetting that over the
telephone it was a pointless gesture. 'But darling Karl,
I'm stranded, you *will* come and drive be back to the
hotel, won't you?'

He was barely audible at the other end of the line,
but from where she stood Sophie heard the deep sound
of his laughter, and felt her senses leap in response to it.
It was easy enough to guess what he said, even before
Flora spoke again. Her manner was much less confident
and Sophie noticed how white her knuckles showed on
the hand that held the receiver.

'Oh but, Karl, you——'

If only she did not feel quite so pleased to hear that
anxious inflection, Sophie thought; she was being almost as malicious as Flora by enjoying her discomfiture
so much, and yet there seemed nothing she could do
about it. Karl knew well enough why Flora was there
and Sophie felt she could never have felt the same
about him again if he had consented to come for her.

The receiver was not so much replaced as slammed
down a moment later, and a glance in Robert's direction showed that he was actually feeling sorry for her.
He went to her, putting a hand on her arm consolingly,
but she snatched angrily away from him. 'Flora, I——'

'Oh, shut up and drive me back!' When she turned
to Sophie her mouth was tight and angry and there
was a bright look about her eyes that was not their
usual glittering hardness but, almost unbelievably,
misty. 'You've managed to worm your way into his
sympathy, but don't bank on it lasting,' she warned in a
flat voice. 'He brought Claude back to me, and that
speaks for itself, doesn't it?'

'I don't know, Flora, does it?'

It was difficult to guess exactly what was going on in Flora's mind, but she looked at Sophie steadily for a moment, then suddenly raised her hand and swung it round until it connected with Sophie's cheek, then she turned and walked to the door, leaving Robert, hoveringly solicitously.

'Oh, Sophie, I'm so sorry about this!'

Her head still spinning from the blow, Sophie put a hand to her face and tried not very successfully to smile at him. 'Why should you be, Robert? You don't know her very well yet, you couldn't know what she's capable of.'

He looked quite incredibly discomfited and she could not imagine what he had in mind as he continued to linger while Flora was outside, already getting into the car. 'I know what she's like, Sophie, but——' He glanced at Flora's yellow blonde head and tall figure just getting into the car and shook his head in a gesture of hopelessness. Then he laughed shortly as he turned away. 'I'm in love with her,' he said. 'It doesn't make sense, does it?'

Sophie stared after him with her lips parted. How could he even consider being in love with someone like Flora when he must know that she could only make him unhappy? For one thing she was far too much engrossed in Karl to even consider another man seriously, and if she were to marry Karl—— She shook her head hastily and closed the door.

'Fräulein Roberts?' Hilde emerged from the kitchen and looked vaguely surprised to find the visitors gone. 'There will be no extra for dinner?'

'No, Hilde.'

Sophie heard the car going off down the hill and shrugged her shoulders in a faintly helpless gesture.

Then she turned and in doing so revealed the mark on her face that Flora's stinging slap had left. Hilde's sparse grey brows expressed surprise for a moment, then she nodded, as if she could put two and two together as well as anyone.

'Your face, Fräulein Roberts—were you struck?'

The smarting cheek would no doubt show a mark for some time, but the last thing Sophie wanted was to make an issue of it, so she shrugged lightly and pulled a face. 'A slight difference of opinion, Hilde, nothing to worry about.'

'The people have gone?'

Hilde was a big woman, even hollowed by the gauntness of old age, and Sophie had the strangest feeling that she would have gone after Flora and dealt with her, if she had still been in the vicinity. She had a strong sense of protectiveness, Karl had told her that much about the old woman, and it seemed she meant to include Sophie in her protection.

'Yes, they've gone, Hilde.'

Hilde murmured something in her own tongue, but she was too curious to let the matter simply stop there, Sophie suspected. Inevitably Lisa would hear about it by morning, and she wondered what she would think about the woman her husband's brother was to marry behaving so violently. She shrugged as Hilde disappeared back into the kitchen, then went along to the playroom to get the boys ready for dinner. Just lately her life seemed to be a series of small crises, and she perhaps ought to be more concerned about it.

'So you had visitors?' Lisa was as curious about the outcome of the visit as the fact of the visit itself, Sophie thought when she brought Lisa's breakfast to her next morning. 'Hilde told me,' she added, as if there could be any doubt.

'Yes, Flora came up with Robert St John to bring my things for me.'

'Ah! That is Bobby St John, the English skier, yes?'

Sophie nodded. She hoped to avoid getting too involved in discussing the visit, and sought a side issue with the hope of drawing Lisa's attention. 'He's staying at the same hotel in Brunnenheim, preparing for the championships next month, like Karl.' She laughed, confessing to divided loyalties. 'I'm torn between the two of them when it comes to giving my support!'

Looking up from pouring herself coffee, Lisa smiled, a small knowing smile that sparkled in her blue eyes. 'Ah, you are torn to decide whether to support the head or the heart, eh? You should be patriotic and cheer for your countryman, you think, but you would rather give your support to Karl. It is a difficult decision, Sophie—what have you decided to do, eh?'

Caught in a trap of her own making, Sophie laughed and shook her head. 'I shall cheer for Robert, I expect, and be patriotic!'

'Oh, but no!' The answer was obviously not one that Lisa expected and the decision puzzled her. 'Let your friend Flora be his champion, since she is obviously— close to him, eh? You must be on the side of Karl, or he will be most hurt, I think.'

It seemed virtually impossible to discuss anything without returning sooner or later to that same subject, and Sophie shrugged uneasily. 'Oh, Flora will be cheering Karl on, definitely.' It struck her suddenly that Lisa should have known that, and she took a moment to consider why she seemed not to recognise the name as a familiar one. 'You probably know Flora, don't you, Lisa? Flora Dauzan—at least you'd know *about* her.'

'I have read about her in the newspapers, I think, and I have heard of her from Karl sometimes. Not a very pleasant woman from what I understand—you worked for her before you came here, did you not?'

The question was so casually put and with such little obvious interest that Sophie could only conclude that Flora was indeed no more than a name to her. Perhaps Karl kept his affairs to himself and said nothing to his family about his plans, although it did not fit in with the new, family-loving image she had discovered during the past few days.

Whatever the reason, Lisa quite clearly knew nothing about the marriage plans he had hinted at, and it was scarcely Sophie's task to enlighten her. It was curious, but it was Karl's business and he would not thank her for discussing it with his sister-in-law.

'Flora's also my cousin, or more correctly my second cousin.'

Lisa blinked her surprise, and it was clear that she suspected something more behind the slap Hilde had reported to her. 'So?'

'I hope you didn't mind them coming here at this particular time, Lisa. If I'd realised they were coming I'd have asked them to put it off until a better time.'

'Oh, but of course you would not!' Lisa sipped her coffee and did not look at her directly, as if she wanted to avoid embarrassing her. 'It was not a very good visit, eh? You quarrelled, you and your cousin?'

'Not exactly quarrelled.' There was little option but to put the incident into its proper perspective, and Sophie laughed as she put her hand to her cheek and grimaced at the memory. 'I said or did something that Flora took exception to, I forget which it was now, and she slapped my face.'

Lisa said something in her own tongue which Sophie suspected was not very complimentary to Flora, and she tore a piece off her breakfast roll with a fierceness that reminded Sophie of Hilde's reaction. 'I wish I had known that this woman was behaving like that in my house, I would have ordered her to go!'

Once more Sophie felt that curiously satisfying sense of belonging, and she felt closer to Lisa, whom she had known for only a few days, than she ever had to Flora. Smoothing down the bedclothes, to help disguise her feelings, she smiled.

'I'm glad you weren't there; I can just imagine what your husband would have to say if my visitors upset you at a time like this! Anyway, what Flora does or says doesn't matter any more. She just wasn't having things her own way, and she isn't used to that!'

'Oh?'

With things as they were between Karl and Flora, even though he had refused to come and drive her back to the hotel, Sophie thought a little discretion was called for. The invitation to confide was too much to resist, but she qualified the blame when she explained the situation, and smoothed the pillows while she did so, to give her hands something to do.

'Poor Flora! First of all I refused to openly quarrel with her, and then Robert turned on her for telling me off. He threatened to drive off without her and she called up Karl at the hotel to ask him to fetch her, and —well, you know Karl. He wouldn't come. It just wasn't her day!'

'And you felt sorry for her?'

Lisa looked unbelieving, but when she thought about it Sophie realised that she quite often felt sorry for Flora. No matter what success she had, and what admiring crowds she gathered around her, Sophie suspected she was quite often more lonely than she was herself. Even the love of her son was given to other people, although she had no one to blame but herself for that.

'I do feel sorry for her sometimes,' Sophie confessed, and Lisa shook her head in confusion over her reasoning.

'I do not understand you,' she said, and Sophie laughed, thinking how much more explicit Karl would have been if he heard her professing sympathy for Flora.

'I'm sure Karl would have put it a lot less politely than that!' she told Lisa. 'He already thinks of me as a rather emotional infant, with more heart than brains!'

Something she caught in Lisa's eyes made her move away from the bed and begin tidying the dressing-table instead, although she was still conscious of being under an interested scrutiny. 'I think you are wrong about that, Sophie,' she said quietly, and bit into the warm bread roll she held between finger and thumb. 'You will see!'

CHAPTER SIX

SOPHIE woke up feeling almost sickeningly excited and took a moment or two to ponder on the prospect the day held. The last four days had been fairly uneventful, apart from the fact that Lisa was now up and getting around a little, although still taking things fairly easily for the time being. The new baby was proving very little trouble and the boys were delighted with her for the most part, although Hugo had one or two reservations about having a girl permanently in the family.

Today promised to be far from run-of-the-mill, and the house would soon be bursting with excitement, for Anton Bruner was coming home. Sophie knew little about him, except that he was Karl's brother and Lisa's husband, and that he was involved in some kind of business dealing at an international level that necessitated his absence from home for long periods at a time. She could so far only guess at the kind of man he was, but today she would have the opportunity of finding out, and last night, for the first time, Sophie had had trouble getting the boys to bed.

Karl was driving his brother from the station, and it was that fact that gave Sophie a greater share in the excitement, she had to admit. He had visited his sister-in-law a couple of times during the last few days, but the visits had been brief; just long enough to check on their combined progress. This time he would be staying for a little longer, and Lisa had passed on the news with the obvious intention of pleasing her.

With the best will in the world there was little Sophie could do to keep the boys as quiet as she would have liked while they bathed and dressed, but their excitement was natural as well as infectious, and even old Hilde shared it while she served them their breakfast, scolding the boys without meaning a word of it, and helping Sophie to dress them in their outdoor clothes so that they could go and watch for the car arriving.

'They're so excited I simply couldn't do a thing to quiet them!' Sophie said as she brought in coffee for her and Lisa, and made a grimace of apology. 'I don't think they'll come to any harm outside, will they?'

'They are used to being out there on their own, they will behave, Sophie, do not worry about them.' Lisa's eyes twinkled at her quizzically. 'You are not finding them too much for you?'

'Oh no, of course I'm not!' The boys were only normally boisterous and, although she had found them rather a handful this morning, she had had no real trouble with them and she did not anticipate any. 'I love being with them, and I think they know it.'

Obviously Lisa was well pleased with the way things were going, for she showed no sign of anxiety. 'You have settled with us so very well, Sophie, that it does not seem possible you have been here such a short time.' She turned and smiled at her once more, with that mischievous gleam in her eyes. 'And today you can share in our excitement, eh?'

They both turned their heads at the same moment, when the boys' chattering burst upon them from the hall, mingled with laughter and the deeper sound of

men's voices, and Sophie's whole being glowed suddenly
as she got to her feet, smoothing down her skirt with
an unconscious gesture of anxiety, while she watched
the door.

'They're here, Lisa!'

The room seemed to be suddenly filled with people
and laughter and the cold smell of mountain air, and
then Lisa too was on her feet, snatched into the arms
of a man who came straight across the big room to her,
with the boys in close pursuit and both chattering at
once. Instinctively taking her eyes from the intimacy
of the moment, Sophie saw Karl standing in the doorway and smiling. He had taken off his outdoor coat
and she was almost startled to realise he was wearing
an ordinary suit with the inevitable high-necked
sweater. He looked taller than ever in light grey, and
a pale blue sweater gave an incredible vividness to his
blue eyes.

Sophie wondered vaguely if she ought to take the
boys with her, but it was a family reunion, and Anton
would surely want to see his sons as well as his new
daughter. Only Karl and Sophie were outside the circle
at the moment, and by common consent they left,
closing the door quietly behind them.

She was unconscious yet of the prickling of tears in
her eyes, but a long forefinger brushing across her
lashes brought the fact home to her, and Sophie laughed
a little unsteadily, ready to defend her emotionalism
if he teased her about it. But instead Karl bent and
kissed her brow as they went through into another,
smaller room at the front of the house, shutting out
the excited chatter from across the hall.

'What a wonderful welcome your brother gets!'

The cold smoothness of Karl's cheek pressed itself

to hers for a moment and he laughed. 'And do I not get a welcome too, Sophie?'

'Yes, of course, the boys——'

Strong fingers dug deep into the top of her arm and she was hugged close to him for a moment. 'I was not speaking of the boys, *Liebling*!'

His body was warm in contrast to the fresh air cold-ness of his face, and crushingly hard when he bound her to him with one arm, arousing the most disturbing responses in her, so that she could scarcely keep her voice steady.

'Well, naturally I'm glad to see you too, Karl.'

'Yes?'

Sensing doubt in his voice, she glanced up at him curiously and so gave him the opportunity he had been seeking. His mouth had a firm hardness that took hers with arrogant confidence and held it for a moment be-fore he let her go. Then the arm about her shoulders was withdrawn and he walked over to the window, standing with his back half turned towards her, and speaking over his shoulder.

'And how are you coping with my rowdy nephews? Are they going to prove too much for you to manage?'

Her head spinning, Sophie answered him in some-thing of a daze, but nevertheless managed to come to the defence of her charges. 'They are not rowdy at all, they're very well behaved!'

Obviously her hasty defence amused him, for he turned around and looked at her, one raised brow commenting on her indignation. 'Ah, so they have won you over, have they? I think you really do have a soft spot for little boys, eh, Sophie?'

She remembered admitting as much to Lisa when she first arrived, and she freely did so now, but talk of little boys inevitably reminded her of Claude, and she could not let the thought pass without asking after him. 'Have you seen anything of Claude, Karl?' She asked knowing that it was inevitable that he had seen Claude's mother, and instinctively put the back of her hand to her lips. 'Is he all right?'

'Yes, he is all right.' He turned right around, his tanned face falling into shadow when he lost the light from the window, and she sensed a taut, cat-like urgency about the lean body with its long legs and broad shoulders. 'Flora had made some kind of temporary arrangement with the hotel, I believe, the rest of the time she is obliged to try and behave as if she was a mother.' His mouth twisted into a mockery of his usual smile and he shook his head. 'It does not suit her very well, but it will do her no harm.'

Sophie's main concern was with how Claude was feeling, being left in charge of various hotel employees, and she caught her breath, looking up at Karl earnestly. 'Oh, Karl, what's going to become of him? I *wish* I hadn't left him!'

'You did not leave him,' Karl reminded her firmly, 'Flora dismissed you!'

'I know, but——'

'It is no use making yourself unhappy by thinking about it, Sophie. It is not—professional to think about your last charge, you must think about now. Claude is Flora's responsibility, and you have Hugo and Hans to care for as well as baby Sophie.' Determined to change the subject, he looked at her enquiringly. 'How *is* my beautiful niece?'

'Oh, she's just beautiful. She's very good and hardly ever cries, and the boys adore her.' She looked up at him, incapable of stilling her concern for Claude, no matter how determinedly Karl refused to discuss it. 'Oh, Karl, if I could just——'

She bit back the plea when he turned his back to her again to resume his study of the front area with its snow-covered bushes and the virgin whiteness of the driveway scribbled over with the darkness of small footprints, deliberately ignoring her appeal. 'I shall be staying here for a few days this time,' he said, as if she had not said anything at all. 'I thought perhaps I could take the boys some time and give you the opportunity to have a break.'

'I'd appreciate that, thank you.'

He turned and smiled at her, a suggestion of mockery in the smile. 'You are not accustomed to having free time, eh?' Her expression was enough to confirm it, and he laughed and shook his head. 'Then you can make plans, perhaps—there is someone you wish to see?'

He had Robert in mind, Sophie realised, and wondered if he was concerned with taking him out of Flora's orbit for a while. It was a surprisingly unwelcome thought and she dismissed it with a swift shake of her head that Karl inevitably misinterpreted.

'No one at all?'

She did not confirm or deny, but left him in no doubt that the idea of some free time was welcome, no matter how she meant to utilise it. 'I'd be very grateful for a few hours to myself, Karl, if you mean it—thank you.'

'Good, then tomorrow I will take charge of the boys and you——' he shrugged carelessly, 'you may do as you please.'

'Will Lisa——' She glanced over her shoulder. 'Shouldn't I ask Lisa first?'

Karl regarded her for a moment with steady, speculative eyes that made her vaguely uneasy, then he shook his head. Curving a big hand about the back of her head, he pulled her towards him and brushed his lips across hers with a lightness that made her shiver. 'Lisa will not mind what you do,' he told her. 'She has Anton and she wants everyone to be as happy as she is, hmm?' Sophie nodded, unable to deny it was true, and Karl smiled, his mouth curved ironically. 'Anton is the lucky one, eh?'

There was a wonderful warm atmosphere about the house now that the Bruner family was complete, and far from being unnoticing Lisa was delighted to hear that Sophie was taking some time off, although Sophie suspected she was less pleased that Karl had volunteered to stand in as mother's help.

They had talked interminably practically ever since Anton came home and, far from being excluded, Sophie was brought into their conversation and encouraged to make her own contribution. They sat facing that fantastic view of the mountains, relaxed in armchairs, just as they had most of yesterday.

Anton was a little younger than Karl and dark-haired. His sense of humour was more boisterous too; a kind of business-man's *bonhomie* that was loud and broad, rather than subtle, but he was a pleasant and friendly man, and Sophie liked him.

His admiration of her was frank and undisguised, and while he sat beside his wife, holding her hand, he winked at his brother and laughed. 'You have excellent taste in young women, Karl, better than you used to have, I think. That yellow-haired creature I saw you with when I left a couple of weeks ago, huh?' He beamed his pleasure at Sophie and teased her with his eyes. 'Sophie is much prettier—you are improving!'

Karl showed no dislike of hearing Flora described as a yellow-haired creature, and Sophie had no doubt that was who Anton meant. He leaned forward in his chair and rested his elbows on his knees, his smile inviting Sophie to join in the surprise he was about to spring on his brother.

'Sophie is Flora's cousin, in fact, Anton. They are both of one family.'

'*Second* cousin, Karl!' she heard herself correcting him shortly, without being quite sure of her reason. 'We're not that close!'

If her attitude surprised him, Karl showed no sign of it apart from a briefly raised brow. 'I am sorry,' he said with mock humility. 'Of course you are nothing at all alike.'

'Nothing,' Anton agreed readily, although he was obviously interested in the fact that she and Flora were cousins, even second cousins. 'It seemed to me that your cousin was somehow—familiar, Sophie, is that possible?'

A swift glance at Karl showed that he evidently meant to leave explanations to her, and Sophie nodded. 'She was quite well known when she was a model; Flora Adams, you've probably heard of her and seen her pictures.' She saw the rest of the picture fall into place for him, when Anton snapped his fingers.

'Flora Dauzan! Of course I should have known when I saw her with Karl that she was something—someone like that!' He was laughing good-naturedly at his brother's penchant for attractive and well-known women and never gave a thought to his earlier suggestions about Sophie. 'You must watch your step, Karl, eh? A wealthy divorcee—she will be looking for another husband!'

Karl said nothing for the moment and before he even looked up, Hilde announced that Robert was there to see Sophie. She did not wait to be asked, but showed him straight in, and from the meaningful look he got it was clear that Hilde remembered his last call and its startling conclusion.

Sophie could not imagine why he was there, and she introduced him rather hesitantly to Lisa and her husband. 'Ah, a—friend of Sophie's, eh?'

Anton's meaning was in no doubt, and Sophie felt a flush of colour warm her cheeks as she invited Robert to sit beside her, studiously ignoring the implication. His fresh and rather plain face looked vaguely embarrassed as he produced a letter from an inside pocket and handed it to her. His name too had been recognised, and he never found it as easy to accept public recognition as Karl did.

'This came for you this morning,' he said. 'I didn't know if it might be important.'

'So you brought it up for me yourself?' His motive seemed even more obscure, and Sophie wished she was not quite so aware of the fact that Karl was watching her curiously. 'That was very good of you, Robert, but you should have had it redirected, not driven all the way up here with it.'

He looked uneasy even though he sat back in his chair and crossed his legs in a seemingly relaxed attitude. It was becoming increasingly obvious that he had hoped to find her alone, and finding her in company instead, he was at a loss to know what to do or say next.

'I—I rather hoped to have a word with you, Sophie.'

'Oh!' More than ever she felt that narrow-eyed, curious gaze of Karl's, and wondered if he suspected something that was as yet unknown to her. It was not easy to simply go somewhere alone with him, but if he seriously wanted to see her in private, she supposed she would have to do something about it. 'I'm sure if you want to speak to me about something personal, Robert, we will be excused for a few minutes.'

'It *is* something rather important.' The plea was irresistible and Sophie nodded. Both she and Robert were half-way out of their chairs when Karl spoke and checked them both.

'Like going back to look after Claude?'

Karl's voice had the softness of silk, but it shivered along Sophie's spine like an icy finger, and Robert was evading his eyes with obvious embarrassment. It was something that should have occurred to Sophie, but it hadn't, and she stared at Robert for a moment rather dazedly.

'*Is* that what it is, Robert?'

It was obvious he did not want to have to admit it in the present company, and especially with Karl watching him so steadily and leaving his views in no doubt. But sooner or later he was bound to give an answer and, after a moment or two, he nodded.

'Flora's going mad, having no one to care for Claude, Sophie. She'll do anything—pay you anything, just as long as you'll come back.'

'No!'

Given no opportunity to answer for herself, Sophie looked at Karl almost unbelievingly as he got to his feet. It was startling to recognise just how angry he was, and she watched him dazedly while he stood looking down at Robert for a moment or two. He had the advantage of several inches in height, and he looked incredibly fierce in a way that she found hard to justify.

'You may tell Flora that Sophie is well suited where she is—she does not wish to come back to her!'

For sheer arrogance his attitude was unbelievable, and even Lisa and Anton were watching him as if they did not quite believe it was happening. Sophie herself was stunned, and yet she could not help feeling sorry for Robert, for she could well imagine with what contempt Flora would hear of his failure as an advocate. Robert shrugged, looking at her rather than Karl, and obviously thinking along the same lines where Flora's opinion was concerned.

'I can't really blame you, Sophie. Not after what happened the last time you and Flora met; I know— I can guess how upset you must have been.'

Putting a hand to her cheek was automatic and quite unconscious, and she did not quite know whether to reassure him by making light of Flora's parting shot, or say nothing. It was Lisa's proxy indignation that decided for her and made Karl narrow his eyes as he looked from one to the other.

'Who would not be upset to have her face slapped?' Lisa demanded indignantly. 'It is not how civilised people behave towards one another, and especially not to a cousin!'

Robert looked discomfited and slightly reproachful, as if he blamed her for telling Lisa about the incident, but Karl was not concerned with anything but the fact that Flora had slapped her, and Sophie could feel the intensity of his gaze on her, searching her flushed cheeks as if he still expected to find some sign of the assault.

'Flora struck you?'

There was an edge on his voice, and he concentrated on her with such intensity that Sophie felt there might have been only the two of them in the room. She nodded without saying anything, not quite sure yet how the slap could be excused; for telling him Flora's reason for hitting out was likely to prove the most embarrassing part of the whole incident.

'It was impulsive, a—a reflex on Flora's part, that's all.' Robert's hasty attempt to justify it was only to be expected, and once more Sophie found herself feeling sorry for him. It was hard to blame him for his loyalty to Flora, no matter how misguided it was. 'You know she didn't mean it, Sophie; she didn't mean to hurt you!'

'*Did* she hurt you, Sophie?'

It was not easy to shake her head when Lisa was watching, and must quite clearly remember the span of Flora's fingers imprinted on her cheek. She shrugged as lightly as she felt able and did not look at him when she answered.

'Not really, it was—just a slap, that's all.'

Behind him she heard Lisa's cluck of disapproval, and guessed that some time in the not too distant future Karl would be regaled with the whole story. At the moment it seemed he was bent on trying to establish reasons, and that was what Sophie had hoped to avoid.

'It was because you were here with me, hmm?' It might have sounded conceited to someone overhearing, but it was the truth and Sophie made no attempt to deny it. Perhaps Lisa and Anton could hear him, or perhaps not; his voice had a softly apologetic gentleness that Robert certainly recognised and was startled by. 'Poor little Sophie; you are the injured innocent, eh?'

'Did I not warn you, Karl?' Anton's hearty voice was threaded with amusement when it broke into the intimacy of the moment, and he laughed as he wagged a warning finger at his brother's heedless back. 'You have been stepping on dangerous ground!'

'I think not!' Karl's voice was cool and flat, but he was looking down at Sophie as if he wondered just what her opinion of his relationship with Flora was. 'I am not committed to anyone and therefore no one, including Flora, has the right to display such violent jealousy!'

'You mean you're not——'

Sophie bit back the rest of the question hastily. Somewhere along the line she had got hold of the wrong idea, and yet she had been so sure that he referred to himself when he spoke of Flora remarrying before very long.

'You do not believe that I am uncommitted, Sophie?'

She shook off the effect of that shiveringly effective voice and tried to answer sensibly. Laughing a little unsteadily, she shook her head. 'Obviously Flora is labouring under the same delusion that I was,' she told him. 'I thought——' She hesitated, conscious of the keen, bright eyes that watched her. 'I thought you and Flora were—getting married.'

'No.' His calmness suggested that he had already guessed what it was she had seen as Flora's excuse. 'I have never said that I will marry Flora and I have given her no cause to think it was even in my mind.'

Sophie said nothing, and for a second or two they stood like a still-life; Karl, Robert and herself. She had said all she could on the subject and so had Karl, apparently, and Robert was too reticent to put into words what showed plainly on his face. He disliked Karl for tossing Flora aside so casually, when he himself would have given his life to be in the same position.

'Mr St John, you will have coffee with us, will you not?'

Lisa's gentle voice broke into the silence, bringing them back to normality, and Sophie saw Robert blink uncertainly for a moment before he nodded. 'Thank you, Madame Bruner, that's very good of you.'

For close on an hour conversation drifted into the commonplace and for the most part concerned skiing; Karl and Robert comparing notes with a kind of wary camaraderie that would probably have developed into something more aggressive if they had not been in the company they were.

It was Robert who brought the visit to an end when he glanced at his wristwatch and whistled silently. 'I'd better think about getting back if I'm to get in some more practice.' He looked at Sophie and half-smiled. 'I need to do a lot better than I have been doing if I'm not to disappoint my supporters at St Moritz next month. And I'm counting on your support, Sophie.'

It had probably been done with the deliberate intention of provoking some kind of reaction from both Karl and Sophie, but it was Karl who took up the challenge, almost inevitably. His eyes showed a faintly malicious glint of laughter when he looked at Sophie and his voice had a teasing overtone of amusement that was irresistible.

'Are you going to desert me, little one?'

Startled into impulsiveness, Sophie shook her head, casting swiftly between him and Robert. 'I'll be cheering for both of you,' she told him, and in her confusion unwittingly quoted Lisa's words. 'I'll follow my heart as well as my head!'

The significance of what she had said dawned on her too late, and she hastily avoided that bright gleaming look of Karl's. 'So?' he said, and put so much meaning into one softly spoken word that Sophie hastily sought to cover her slip.

'I have to cheer for Robert, of course, being from my own country!' She turned and smiled at Robert, getting to her feet when he did. 'I wonder if you'd be good enough to drive me down into Brunnenheim with you, Robert, would you? There's something I want to get that I can't get in the village. If you wouldn't mind.'

'No, of course not—come by all means.' Quite clearly the request had taken him by surprise, and he looked vaguely uneasy, as if he too was aware of Karl's scrutiny. 'Are you ready to go now?'

'I need a couple of minutes to fetch a jacket, and I'll be with you. I won't keep you long.'

'Sophie? I can drive you just as well, if you wish to go. Why did you not say?'

She was already turned away when Karl questioned her, and she half-turned to look over her shoulder at him. 'You've promised to take care of the boys for me,' she reminded him, with a sense of satisfaction she did not quite understand. 'I cán go with Robert, thank you, Karl.'

'And how will you get back?' It hadn't occurred to her how she was going to get back, but almost inevitably Karl had a ready solution. 'Do not worry, when you are ready, I will come and fetch you.'

Something in his manner, almost as if he did not trust her out of his sight, Lisa's bright mischievous eyes, and Anton's unmistakable smile all contributed to make her react as she did. Leaving Robert to make his good-byes, she went to collect her coat. 'Oh, there's no need for you to,' she told Karl as she went. 'I'll get a cab.'

She had collected her jacket and pulled a hat on over her unruly hair and was on her way downstairs once more when she saw Karl standing in the hall waiting for her. He stood at the foot of the stairs, with an elbow resting on the rail and a thumb tapping his teeth thoughtfully, and he did not smile when she ventured a brief one of her own.

'You *will* come back, Sophie?'

Startled, she looked at him uncomprehendingly for a second, before she grasped his meaning, then she flushed, using both hands to tug the woollen hat she wore down over her ears with unnecessary force. 'Of course I'll come back; what makes you think I wouldn't?'

He did not answer right away but studied her flushed and slightly indignant face for a second or two before he smiled—a wry, half-apologetic smile that showed in his eyes as a bright gleam and misshaped his wide mouth.

'Because Flora will not hesitate to use Claude if she is as desperate as St John claims she is. I know you, little Sophie; if you are faced with Claude's appealing face and the thought of his being unhappy, you will stay with him no matter what lies in store for you where Flora is concerned.'

It was true, more true than she cared to admit, and she hastily shook her head. 'I'm not going to see either Flora or Claude,' she told him. 'I'm going to try and find something for little Sophie—a christening present. I don't know if you have the tradition here.'

'We do.' He was smiling, partly appeased, but not

altogether, it was obvious. 'It is very kind of you, Sophie, and Lisa will be delighted that you have thought of it.'

'And you really thought I'd leave Lisa in the lurch like that? You still don't have a very good opinion of me, do you, Karl?'

Her bottom lip pouted reproachfully and, after a moment, he put a long forefinger to it and pulled it down, then bent his head and kissed her, one hand curved about her jaw. 'Just come back from Brunnenheim, little one, that is all I ask of you at the moment.' Sophie nodded, not trusting herself to speak, and he held her tightly for a second with his hand about her face. 'Promise?'

'I promise, Karl—I do wish you'd trust me!'

'I trust you!' He kissed her again, just as the door of the sitting-room opened and Robert came out into the hall with Anton. Seeing them, Robert looked momentarily embarrassed, but Anton was beaming uninhibitedly. 'Give my love to Brunnenheim!' Karl whispered, and Sophie turned swiftly away.

Brunnenheim was pleasantly familiar, but Sophie had already decided that she would not want to exchange it for the splendid but curiously cosy isolation of Schläfing, and she pondered on how much had happened since she last walked along the busy main street of the village.

Having sought out her favourite café, she sat at one of its small tables enjoying a large and very rich *Gugelhupf* whose hollow centre was stuffed with whipped cream. She had meant to resist the temptation of various pastries and cakes, but there was something about Swiss cafés that was irresistible.

The street outside was thronging with people, and she eyed them casually as she sat there, until a small familiar face caught her eye. A small and rather sober face topped by a red wool hat, large dark eyes eagerly seeking a favourite cake as he came into the café with a middle-aged woman.

For a moment or two he was too engrossed in choosing his pastry to be aware of anything else, but then, having made his choice, he looked around and saw her. For a moment Sophie thought he was going to burst into tears, but then he looked up at the woman he was with instead, and tugged at her hand, urging her across to where Sophie was sitting.

'Sophie! Sophie!'

'Hello, Claude.' There was nothing she could do to stop the sudden misting of her eyes, and the woman with Claude was looking a little suspicious. 'It's all right,' Sophie assured her, 'I'm a distant cousin of Claude's—I used to take care of him.'

'Ah!' Enlightened, the woman was a little less suspicious, but she still kept a firm hand on her charge, and declined Sophie's invitation to join her. 'You will excuse, please, but we have to go.'

'I want to talk to Sophie!' Claude's bottom lip trembled, and it appalled Sophie to realise that if he cried she would probably be unable to stop herself doing so as well. 'Sophie!'

'Just a minute?' She looked at the woman every bit as appealingly as Claude looked at her, and after a moment's thought, the woman shrugged plump eloquent shoulders and sat down at the table.

Tugging his hand free, Claude came round to stand beside Sophie, his dark eyes more appealing than she had ever seen them, and tugging at her heart-strings as she shook her head over a request to go back to the hotel with them.

'I have a new little baby to take care of, Claude, as well as Hugo and Hans.'

'You like them better than me?'

'Oh no, of course not, but—Well, I have a different job now, and I work for Madame Bruner instead of your *maman*. Do you understand?'

'Karl has gone too!' Claude was too upset to think of anything but his own unhappiness. 'And I don't want Uncle Bobby for my father, Sophie—I want Karl!'

Sophie blinked hard and there was a curious stiffness about the smile she managed to produce. It was ironic, she thought, that something that gave her a certain pleasure should make Claude so unhappy. He had been so anxious to have Karl for his stepfather, and now it seemed there was no chance of it ever happening.

'I'm sorry, Claude, but—well, things don't always work out the way we want them to. It just happens, no one can do anything about it.'

She wished there was something she could do to erase that look of reproachful uncertainty from his face, and after a second she remembered the presents she had bought for the boys. Reaching into her bag, she produced the small clockwork clown she had meant for Hans, and handed it to him.

'I have a little present for you!' She wound up the toy and put it down on the table, and for a second or two Claude was distracted enough to smile. 'Isn't he funny?'

He took the toy and tried to rewind it and, when he could not, the woman with him gently took it from him and wound it. 'So!' She set it down on the table in front of him and looked across at Sophie with unmistakable meaning. It was her opportunity to go, while he was occupied with his new toy, and Sophie took it, though not without a twinge of guilt.

'You'll have fun with that, Claude, won't you? Why don't you sit here and play with it for a while, and I'll finish my shopping, eh?'

Claude nodded without speaking. He knew she wasn't coming back, but at the moment he preferred not to recognise it and chose instead to allow himself to be distracted by a new toy. He did not even look up when she hovered for a moment, wondering if she dared drop a kiss on top of his head before she went, but she decided that personal contact was likely to break down his barrier of self-delusion, and instead she bit hastily on her lip and walked out of the café.

CHAPTER SEVEN

THE boys had been put to bed and Sophie was meant to be joining in the general conversation, but somehow her mind continually returned to her last glimpse of Claude, playing with the toy clown she had given him, pretending he did not mind her going away without him.

Anton was doing most of the talking, for he was an inveterate story-teller and kept his audience amused for hours on end without tiring. Usually Sophie enjoyed his occasionally colourful yarns, but this evening she found it impossible to concentrate for very long.

Karl was seated next to her and it became clear after a time that he had noticed her absent-mindedness, for he glanced at her from time to time and frowned curiously. Stretched out in an armchair, as he was now, he always looked so completely at ease, with his long legs crossed at the ankles and his blond head resting on the back of the chair, eyes half closed.

Anton was relating some incidents during his last trip, to Lisa, and as yet had not noticed how distracted she was, but after several moments Karl reached across and stroked a long finger across the back of Sophie's hand, smiling when she looked up swiftly. Dismissing Claude's image once more, she managed a smile, but it was so obviously contrived that Karl frowned over it.

He sat up in his chair and leaned towards her on one of the arms, so that she stiffened herself in preparation for the inevitable questions. The toy clown she had given to Claude, she had replaced with another for Hans, and so far she had said nothing about seeing Claude while she was out. Now it was almost inevitable, she feared, and wished it was not so easy to remember that unhappy little face.

'What is troubling you, Sophie?'

He spoke quietly, below the pitch of Anton's voice, and Sophie glanced at him only briefly, then shook her head. 'Nothing,' she denied, and Karl frowned.

'Then why do you look so unhappy, *hein*?' When she did not answer he went on to form his own opinions. 'You have seen Flora!' He did not raise his voice, but something in his tone must have attracted the attention of the others, for Lisa was looking from one to the other curiously as Anton came to the end of his story and realised at last that Lisa had been the only one listening.

'No, I haven't, Karl! I told you I wouldn't!' The tanned features looked to be chipped from teak as he gazed at her for a moment, deciding whether or not to believe her, and Sophie's hands curled tightly on the arm of her chair. 'I saw Claude, but I had no option. He came in to the same café I was in, and he saw me.'

'Claude?'

Sophie knew what he was asking, and shook her head. 'There was a middle-aged woman with him. One of the hotel maids, I think—I thought I recognised her.'

'And it has upset you?' He knew it had upset her and, either heedless or unaware of his brother's interest, he leaned across and folded his long fingers over hers where they lay tightly rolled on the chair arm. 'Oh, Sophie, you are too soft-hearted, *Liebling*! Claude is Flora's child, she must look after him, it is her responsibility!'

'How do you explain something like that to a four-year-old child?' She sounded quite uncharacteristically bitter, and when she remembered what else had been upsetting Claude, she could not refrain from mentioning it, no matter how unwise it might prove to be. 'He's upset about you too; he misses you, Karl!'

'I know that he must do.' He did not impatiently dismiss the idea as she half expected him to. 'But he is young, Sophie, and he will learn to—love other people in time.'

'Oh, you make it sound so easy—so—so unimportant, and it isn't—not to Claude! He thought you were going to be his father; he spoke of nothing else for the past few weeks. Next to learning to ski it was what he wanted most!'

'I know that too.'

Sophie knew she was being almost childishly reproachful in her anxiety about Claude, but she could almost feel his loneliness as if it was her own, and she wanted to cry when she thought of him deprived of the only two people who had cared about him.

Lisa and Anton were silent, sitting close together and holding hands, waiting, without appearing to intrude, to see what was going to happen, and Lisa was anxious, she could tell. Anxious because she hated to see anyone unhappy when she was so happy herself.

'Sophie!' Karl's voice once more brought her back to calm reason. 'What would you have me do? Marry Flora so that Claude may have his way and have me for his stepfather?'

'No, of course not, that's—silly!'

'Then I do not see what else I can do about it, little one.'

Put like that it made her outburst seem all the more unreasonable, and she shook her head helplessly. It had only now occurred to her that her mood was affecting everyone else as well, and she glanced across at Lisa and Anton and pulled a wry face by way of apology.

'Lisa, I'm so sorry, I didn't mean to bring someone else's problems into your home, please forgive me.' She shrugged uneasily and tried to laugh off her mood, but Lisa as ever, understood and did not blame her.

'But of course you are concerned with that poor child, Sophie. You have the soft heart, as Karl says, but I understand how it is you feel; it is natural in a woman.'

'It is also pointless!' Karl decreed firmly, and Anton, rather surprisingly, laughed.

'But it is not for their soft hearts that we love them, Karl? Or are you too accustomed to the hardness of your yellow-haired fashion model, eh?'

For a moment Karl said nothing, but his eyes moved slowly and searchingly over Sophie's face and came to rest at last on the tremulous softness of her mouth, then he smiled slowly. 'Perhaps you are right,' he allowed softly, and squeezed her fingers. 'It has always been my regret that I have never known quite how to influence Sophie, and she does not help me at all.'

'Perhaps because I don't want to be—to be influenced!'

Her objection was as much to the way her own senses were responding to his apparent desire to influence her, whatever that implied, as to the remark itself. He sat up in his chair now, leaning forward with his elbows resting on his knees and his big strong-looking hands clasped together. More and more lately she had begun noticing things about him, just as she had three years ago, and the realisation made her not only uneasy but impatient with what she saw as her own weakness.

Fair brows below a swathe of silky blond hair were drawn close in one of his disapproving frowns, and she could sense Lisa's interest in the exchange. 'Forgive me if my English is less than perfect, Sophie, but I think you know I do not mean that literally!'

There was an edge on his voice as sharp as steel and she felt a flush of colour as she looked down at her folded hands rather than at him. 'I'm sorry.'

'Oh, Sophie!' Regardless of his brother and Lisa, well within earshot, he leaned closer and clasped her hands in his, squeezing her fingers hard, as if by contact he hoped to convey his true feeling. 'Why will you so often misunderstand me, eh? Will you not for once come at least part way to meet me, instead of—putting up this barrier?'

'Karl——'

The sudden shrill of the telephone in the hall stopped her short, and a moment later Hilde put her head around the door and announced that the call was for Sophie. Puzzled, she frowned for a moment, then looked rather vaguely at Karl, with a half-formed suspicion in her mind as she got to her feet. It seemed unlike Flora to go to the lengths of calling her up and asking her to come back and work for her, and yet somehow——

'It is Madame Dauzan, Fräulein Roberts,' Hilde said, and Sophie saw the swift upward jerk of Karl's head.

His narrow-eyed gaze followed her across the big room, and she wondered if he too had the same suspicion in mind. The telephone was immediately outside the door and she did not close it behind her because in some odd way it made her feel just a little less vulnerable knowing that Karl could hear what was being said.

'Hello, Flora?' Her hands were trembling and the realisation appalled her so that she tightened her grip on the receiver to try and prevent it.

'You sneaking, underhand little bitch! You have exactly an hour to bring him back and then I go to the police!' The words crackled against her ear, high-pitched and hysterical, and at first Sophie wondered if she was imagining them. 'Do you hear me?'

It was Flora, there was no mistaking the voice, but what on earth was wrong with her, Sophie could not even guess. 'Flora, I can't imagine what's wrong—has something happened?'

'You know well enough what's happened! You came down here, inveigled your way into his favour by giving him some silly toy, then took him away with you!'

Something in the pit of Sophie's stomach tightened like an icy spring, and she needed a moment to recover her breath, when she spoke again her voice was carefully under control but still not quite steady. 'Flora, has—has something happened to Claude?'

That small unhappy face flashed once more into her mind, and she held the receiver with almost breaking strength, trying to bring back reason. Flora, if she understood her correctly, was accusing her of taking Claude away, but if she hadn't taken him then—She caught her breath, listening to Flora's hysterical outburst in stunned silence. 'You know better than I do what's happened to him! The woman who was looking after him told me you saw them in Brunnenheim this afternoon, and only hours later he's gone!'

It was so difficult to think clearly, and Sophie put a hand to her forehead. It must be seven hours or more since she had seen Claude with the hotel maid, and surely he could not have been gone all that time. 'But it was hours ago that I saw him, Flora! You must know I wouldn't do anything as—as heartless as taking him away from you without saying anything!'

'I know you'd do anything to get back at me for slapping you! You could easily have come to the hotel and taken him after the maid left him—people here know you, you'd have no trouble getting in.'

'He was alone?' The idea of Claude sitting alone in his room made her feel like crying, but she must do something more constructive than weep for him at the moment. 'Oh, Flora, he could be anywhere!'

'He's with you, of course he is!' Flora was trying desperately to convince herself, Sophie realised, no matter how wild the idea was—the alternative did not bear thinking about. 'He'd go anywhere with you, and you know it!'

It was sheer panic that drove her on, and the same panic already stirring in her own breast let Sophie make allowances for her. 'He isn't here with me, Flora, he really isn't. I don't know where he is.'

'Liar! You're doing it to spite me, you've *got* to be!'

'Flora, please, don't! I'll—I'll come down and see you—see if I can help. I just don't know what to suggest, but he can't have gone far.'

'In four hours?'

The shivering chill that coursed along her spine was

diminished suddenly by contact with a firm warm body that pressed close for a moment before a hand reached round and took the telephone from her unresisting fingers. Instinct made her lean back against him for a moment and close her eyes, and Karl's mouth pressed lightly and very briefly to her neck before he took over the conversation.

'Flora? This is Karl—what has happened that you ring Sophie at this hour and frighten her so?'

Whatever Flora said was only audible in part to Sophie as she stood beside Karl, one thumb pressed anxiously between her teeth, but she heard the accusation she hurled at him quite clearly. 'Why aren't you here when I need you, Karl? Why do you have to go all the way up there in the mountains when I need you down here with me?'

'Flora, Sophie has already told you that Claude is not here. No one here has seen him since Sophie spoke to him in a café earlier today.'

This time the words were not clear enough to carry and Sophie watched Karl's face anxiously while he listened. He looked so serious, and his blue eyes had darkened to something less than their usual brilliance, so that she slid a hand under his arm and pressed her fingers comfortingly into the flesh beneath a thick wool sweater.

'Tell me everything that happened, Flora, and do not become hysterical, that will not help at all. You are quite certain that he is not still somewhere in the hotel and hiding from you?'

'Of course I'm sure! It's been searched from top to bottom and he isn't here!' She still seemed to see no blame attached to her own behaviour. 'It's four hours, Karl, and that stupid woman didn't say a word about seeing Sophie until just now. Of course I knew at once where he was then!'

'Well, you are mistaken! You say you have not seen him since four hours ago?'

'The hotel maid saw him four hours ago. I saw him at breakfast—he had his lunch in his room and then one of the maids took him out.'

Karl's mouth was set tight and there was a bright hard gleam in his eyes, but even so his next words struck Sophie as incredibly harsh in the circumstances. 'You are without doubt the worst mother in the world, Flora, and if Claude has been kidnapped it is your fault; but we must think of the boy.'

'Kidnapped!' Sophie clung to his arm, looking at him with wide, incredulous eyes. 'Oh, Karl, he—he surely can't be!'

Ignoring Flora's hysterical babbling at the other end of the line, he put an arm around Sophie's shoulders and hugged her close. 'It has to be taken into consideration with a child like Claude Dauzan, little one.' He kissed her brow reassuringly. 'But I do not think it is so, I think it is more likely that he has wandered off, feeling himself to be abandoned.'

'Oh no!'

Karl returned to his telephone conversation, saying much the same thing to Flora as he had to Sophie, but adding some advice that he could only hope Flora would follow. 'If someone has taken him it is a matter for the police, but if he has gone off alone somewhere, then it is important that he is found quickly or he could die of exposure, a child so small.'

He was deliberately making things sound as bad as possible to make Flora understand what her neglect had come to, Sophie realised, but all the same she shivered in horror at the idea of Claude being out there in the cold and the dark, lost and frightened and definitely in danger unless he was found quite quickly.

'I will come down and help, and so will Anton, I know. If we start to search this end it may help, but you must set the wheels in motion for a search party from the village. Robert St John will help, he knows the procedure.' He listened for a second, tight-lipped impatiently frowning over the delay, then cut short the appeal. 'Time is important, Flora—you do your part and we will do ours! Goodbye!'

He slammed the receiver down heavily, then stood for a second with one hand in a pocket, the other still encircling Sophie's shoulders, holding her close to his side. 'I must see Anton!' Releasing her suddenly, he went striding back into the sitting-room until Sophie called after him.

'I'm coming as well, Karl!' Seeing the look in his eyes when he turned, she shook her head firmly. 'Don't say I can't, because I'm coming! I can't stay here when Claude's missing and he could be out there—oh God!' She shivered, whispering the prayer automatically as she followed him into the room. 'I'll tell Lisa, she'll understand.'

'And you think I will not?'

His arm came around her shoulders as she caught up with him and she managed a brief and rather unsteady smile when she looked up at him. 'I think you do,' she told him, and meant it.

Sophie thought she had never seen Flora so upset, though how much of it was genuine and how much put on for Karl's benefit she made no attempt to guess. At the sight of Karl she gave a cry and rushed towards him, regardless of the fact that the hotel lounge was crowded with people. Her intention had been to throw herself into his arms, Sophie had little doubt, but the manoeuvre was successfully countered by two strong hands that gripped her arms firmly and held her at nearly arms' length while she babbled breathlessly.

More conscious of being surrounded by other people, Karl took her arm and guided her into an alcove around a corner, where it was quieter and they were unlikely to cause a disturbance; and Anton and Sophie followed.

'You have only yourself to blame for what has happened, Flora!' The words were scarcely comforting, but at least they dragged Flora out of her self-pity, and she looked at him with angry, reproachful eyes.

She showed no sign of tears and Sophie wondered if the situation was really affecting her as much as she would like Karl to believe. Even at a time like this she had taken the trouble to make the most of her appearance.

Her yellow-blonde hair that Anton had commented on was freshly tended and coaxed into its usual carefully casual style, and her make-up was recently renewed and immaculate as ever. She wore slim black suede boots and a perfectly fitted après-ski suit in black and gold that showed off both her colouring and the boyish slenderness of her figure.

Brushing a finger-tip across her darkened lashes as if to remove a tear, she gazed up at Karl, completely ignoring Sophie, although Anton drew an interested glance. 'You're quite heartless, aren't you?' she accused, and assumed that embarrassingly familiar little-girl look of reproach that Sophie hated, though it was clear she knew it was wasted on Karl. 'I'm frantic with worry and don't know who to turn to, and all you do is blame me!'

'You could turn to Robert St John for one, he would help you and be glad to be allowed to.'

Flora looked at him for a second through her thick lashes, speculating quite openly on his response. 'Karl darling, you're not jealous of poor Bobby, are you?'

'Not in the least, Flora, but he is more than willing to help, and we are going to need all the help we can muster to find Claude if he has gone off on his own.' His cool rejection of her made even Sophie flinch, and she saw the way Flora bit hard on her lower lip. 'You have informed the authorities, of course?'

Flora shook her head. Her lower lip was pouted sulkily and she was obviously unprepared for such cavalier treatment. Karl's only concern was for Claude's safety, and he left her in no doubt of it. 'I haven't told anyone yet, except you, I don't want it made official until we've made absolutely sure we can't find him ourselves. If Rudi hears about it, I'll lose control of Claude, and——'

'And ultimately of the Dauzan millions! *Umgotteswillen!*' Karl snatched his hands from her, as if the very touch of her was distasteful to him. 'Unless you agree to the authorities being informed, there is nothing I can do—I will not work blindly!'

'Karl!' The steadiness of his eyes brought a flush to her face, and after a second or two she shook her head and yielded. 'All right—I'll get someone to ring whoever it is I have to ring.'

Karl turned to his brother. 'We must do that first, Anton, and then we can begin to search.'

Anton nodded agreement, but Flora, still not ready to face the obvious, looked up at Karl appealingly, a hint of that little-girl sulkiness still lingering about her mouth to reproach him. 'What about me, Karl darling—what can I do?'

Karl gave her a look of such unconcealed contempt that she coloured furiously under her make-up, then he turned his back on her. 'You can go and amuse yourself in the bar, darling Flora, while we go and find your son!'

Sophie had said nothing in all this time and Flora might have been unaware of her presence for all the notice she took of her, but when Karl automatically took her arm as they moved away, Flora's sharp, resentful voice followed them. 'What is *she* doing here? If anyone's responsible for Claude being missing it's her!' No one turned and Flora's voice rose shrilly. 'Karl!'

Sophie, through her contact with him, could feel how tense he was as he half-turned, and she saw the glittering anger in his eyes. Karl could not easily forgive the neglect of a child, and particularly by the child's own mother. 'Sophie will be of use in the search, Flora, and that does not imply that she has any idea of Claude's whereabouts. Now please allow us to start looking for your son, too much time has been lost already.'

Flora subsided, beaten, and they left her standing in the quiet annexe of the hotel lounge alone; a curiously pathetic figure for all her glamorous trappings. Faced with the loss of something, or someone, she really wanted, she had such a touching air of loneliness that Sophie wondered if she should have stayed with her.

'You were very hard on her.' Anton's hands were thrust into the pockets of his jacket, and he looked at his brother over the top of Sophie's head as they walked either side of her out into the street.

His darkly tanned face set into an expression of stubborn anger, Karl did not look at him, but kept his eyes steadily ahead where the light gleamed out on to the snowy pavements. His bright hair was covered by a woollen cap, and his broad shoulders hunched while he walked, giving him an even bulkier look than the padded jacket already did.

Sophie knew he was fond of Claude; not in the same admittedly sentimental way that she was herself, but just because he was a child and therefore vulnerable. He had looked as if he actually hated Flora back there in the hotel, and for a moment she had sympathised with her selfish cousin as she never had before. Whatever Flora's faults, she had very genuinely strong feelings for Karl, though whether she loved him was another matter.

It was several moments before he answered his brother's accusation, and then he shrugged his shoulders as if he shrugged off something he preferred not to recognise. 'She has been hard on a great many people,' he said in a flat cold voice, 'including Sophie. I do not think Flora can claim permanent immunity from the more disagreeable facts of life.'

'You think she does not care for her son?'

To Anton the thought was inconceivable, and Karl gave him a wry half-smile above Sophie's head. 'As much as she cares for anyone but Flora Dauzan,' he allowed.

Anton probed deeper. 'And Karl Bruner?' he suggested softly, and once more Karl's broad shoulders shrugged off something that was seemingly unwelcome.

'Claude would be so much happier and better cared for in the care of his grandmother, the Comtesse,' he said. 'The pity is that there is nothing anyone can do about having him returned to her—events alone can do that.'

There was a sense of urgency about the three of them as they made their way along the brightly lit street, and Sophie's fingers were tightly rolled into fists in the pockets of her jacket as she walked between the two men. It was instinctive when she glanced up at the shimmering dominance of the Schillenberg, already bathed in moonlight and somehow showing a more sinister aspect than ever before.

'Karl.' Blue eyes were turned enquiringly on her, almost as if he had forgotten she was there with them, and a half-smile encouraged her to go on. 'It's probably a silly idea, but I'm wondering about where Claude would go if he has gone off on his own somewhere.' Once more her gaze went involuntarily to the snowy mass of Schillenberg, and she shivered. 'You know how fond he was of riding up to the Maiden's Tower in the cable-car, would he have——'

'But of course!' A hand squeezed hers tightly. 'He would very likely go to some place where he was happy, somewhere like the Mädchen Turm where you so often took him. You are a clever girl, little one, to think of it!'

The glow that his commendation gave her was diminished somewhat by his almost paternal manner, but this was no time to be touchy about attitudes, and she put forward another suggestion without hesitation. 'I could go along to the terminus and ask if he's been seen taking the cable-car to the summit, while you and Anton see the police, or whoever it is who sets the official wheels in motion. It will save time and——' She glanced again at the chilling hugeness of the mountain with its deceptive air of tranquillity, and hastily swallowed on a sudden rush of panic. 'There's so little time!'

The suggestion was taken up without hesitation, and she left the two men, to hurry on towards the cable-car terminus, practically deserted at this time of day, as it had been nearly two weeks ago when Karl had tried to whisk her away to join one of Flora's parties. It could even have been the same man who stood behind his glass partition and looked at her curiously when she questioned him about a small boy alone.

'I have seen no children this evening, *Fräulein*.' His lined face, further gnarled by the harshness of the overhead lights, looked concerned. 'A child is lost, *Fräulein*?'

'He's missing from his hotel room,' Sophie explained, and realised suddenly just how little she knew of the actual circumstances. 'The hotel has been searched, but he still hasn't been found, and it's more than four hours now since anyone saw him.'

'The authorities——' he began, but Sophie shook her head.

'His mother hasn't told them, but they're being informed now. It's been so long.' She shivered at the thought of what the delay could mean to Claude's safety. 'I thought he might have come here and taken the car up to Mädchen Turm, it was his favourite ride.'

'I am sorry, *Fräulein*.'

Sophie smiled, rather unsteadily. 'It was just a thought,' she said, and turned away disconsolately. 'Thank you anyway.'

'*Fräulein, warten Sie ein Moment!*' Hopefully Sophie turned back. The man was leaning out from his glass cage and signalling to her with one hand. 'You said that it is four hours that the child has been gone?'

'That was the last time he was seen by anyone who knew him.'

'If that is so, then it is possible that my——' He groped for a moment for an unfamiliar word while Sophie burned with impatience. 'The man who was in this place before me was here for two of the last four hours, *Fräulein*. Perhaps he saw the child.'

It was a slender thread, but Sophie grasped it with both hands, thanking the man and trembling in her anxiety to find Karl and put even the smallest scrap of information into his hands. 'If you can tell me where I can find him,' she urged. 'We could ask him—please.'

He gave it a moment's thought, then wrote down an address on a fragment of paper and pushed it through the opening to her. Stopping only to thank him, Sophie hurried off. Anton and Karl would be at the police station, or at the rescue headquarters, and if she could let them know that she was following up the address she had been given it would all save time.

She was on her way to the police station when she noticed the name on a small side turning off the main street, and checked it with the paper she held in her hand. If the man she had just spoken to spoke passable English, almost certainly his daytime counterpart would, and if she could take proof positive that Claude had gone up to the Maiden's Tower, then it would be a big help.

The street was less well lit than the one she had just left, but she found the address easily enough. The man was as eager to help as she hoped he would be, but he took some time to remember a child alone. There had been a child, but he had thought him in the company of a young couple—it could have been his mistake, they had not spoken to the little boy at all.

It was enough for Sophie, she left the neat little house and hurried back to the terminus. Claude loved the café just below the summit, he would happily sit there for hours if she let him, so it was just possible that he was sitting there now, lost and alone, and wondering if anyone was ever coming to fetch him.

The man in the office willingly agreed to tell Karl and Anton where she had gone, and she began the long, slow ride up the mountain side, nervously curling and uncurling her hands at the unhurried pace of the climb. Claude would be sure to wait, if he was still at the top; he would not know where else to go. She consoled herself with that as she watched the lights of the café draw nearer, and when the doors slid open at the top she almost ran from the car and into the dazzling warmth of the glass-walled building.

'A small boy,' she asked the question breathlessly of the girl behind the counter bar. 'Have you seen a small boy with dark hair and eyes, about so high?'

She prayed the girl spoke English, and breathed a sigh of relief when she answered. 'There was a small boy, *Fräulein*, a short time ago.'

'Alone?' The girl looked puzzled, then shrugged, obviously not aware of the seriousness of the question. 'Was he alone or was he with someone, this little boy you saw?'

'With someone, *Fräulein*.'

Sophie's heart sank and she looked at the girl anxiously. 'You're sure?'

Frowning, the girl nodded, though she was less certain, Sophie could see, just as the cable-car man had been, when it came to the point. 'He left with some people, *Fräulein*, I think he was with them.'

Sophie stood for a moment feeling utterly hopeless. She did not know what to do next. If Claude had returned to Brunnenheim in the cable-car, then the search had to begin from the beginning. 'Thank you.' She went out into the cold air, shivering involuntarily as she pulled the collar of her jacket up around her ears. She could only hope that Karl and Anton were not already on their way up in the next car.

Walking to the corner of the building, where she had managed to conceal herself on the night Karl brought her up there, she stood for a second and tried to put herself in Claude's place. But her mind could not hope to follow the impulses of an unhappy four-year-old and she shrugged after a moment and strode back in the opposite direction, standing and staring down at the snowy slopes that swept down into the valley via that dark belt of protective trees.

It looked so lonely at night. Its beauty was lost on her in the present circumstances and she could only think of Claude and how unhappy he must have been to venture out alone. Maybe he had thought to find her, to see her again, or to see Karl. The moonlight made patches of darkness in the snow, casting shadows where there was nothing to throw a shadow, and it was deceptive; but what she noticed was not a deception, she felt sure, and her blood ran cold suddenly as she looked at the glistening cold surface of the snow.

Leading off from the end of the platform on to the mountainside were small, deep footprints that petered out when there was no longer light to see them by. Sophie put her hand to her mouth and stared at the marks with blank disbelief. 'Claude!'

CHAPTER EIGHT

SOPHIE was too stunned to do anything for a second or two. She could only stand and stare at the trail of small footprints in the snow, leading out into the darkness beyond the perimeter of the yellow light from the café windows. Heaven knew what had possessed Claude to venture beyond the comfort of light and warmth, but if he was out there on the mountainside he had to be found very quickly, or the consequences could be tragic.

Turning quickly, she hurried back into the café, and the girl behind the bar looked up curiously. Sophie wasted no time, there was none to waste; she glanced at the telephone behind the bar-counter. 'Will you get help, please, quickly?' Quick to grasp the urgency of her appeal, the girl nodded. 'Claude—the little boy I was asking you about, has apparently walked off down the mountain, I've spotted his tracks from the corner of the building.' She pointed firmly in the right direction, so that there could be no mistake, and once more the girl nodded understanding.

'I will telephone at once, *Fräulein*!'

'I'm going to see if I can spot him, or get to him.'

'*Ach*, no, that is most unwise!'

A lifetime in touch with such emergencies had made the Swiss girl more aware of the dangers and more practical in her outlook. But to Sophie the thought of

simply waiting around for someone else to come and
look for Claude when she was there on the spot was
unacceptable, and she shook her head.

'I'm just going to try and locate him—will you get
what help you can, please?'

To her relief the girl offered no further argument,
but was already picking up the telephone when Sophie
turned back towards the door. Outside once more,
she shivered, and not only from the cold wind that
stung her face like a slap when she faced into it. The
mass of snow on the mountain slopes could envelop a
child as small as Claude and leave no trace but those
pathetically small footprints.

Her own courage almost failed, faced with the vastness of it, shimmering like powdered crystal in the light
from the windows. Following literally in Claude's footsteps she began the descent and found it unexpectedly
gradual at first; he had traversed the slope rather than
taken the direct way down, and in a way she found
that comforting. Beyond the aureole of yellow light
from the café, however, the going was more difficult and
the footprints harder to discern among the shadows of
ridged and drifted snow.

The moon was in its last quarter and it gave a lot less
light than she could have wished, but at least the vastness of the snowy mountainside reflected what light
there was, even though it deepened the shadows.

'Claude!' Standing quite still, she listened for
another sound above the hammering urgency of her
own heartbeat and the soft, lonely voice of the wind.
'Claude!'

There was no answer, but there had been so much delay, heaven knew how far he could have gone. Across
the valley it was almost possible to make out the road

along which she and Claude had driven with Karl, or
so she told herself. It helped to still the growing panic
she felt, to think that Schläfing and the comfort of
Anton and Lisa's home was almost in sight.

'Claude!'

Raising her eyes from an identifiable footprint to
locate the next one, she missed her footing, and a cry
was torn from her throat as she was tossed helplessly over
and over down over the powdery snow. The only thing
in her mind as she bumped and rolled down the slope
was how far it was down to the barrier of pine trees.
The possibility of starting an avalanche with her fall
did not occur to her until a second before she was
brought up short by a half buried tree stump and had
the breath completely knocked out of her for a
moment.

For a second or two she lay with her stomach pressed
against the tree stump, gasping and feeling slightly
sick. Then, moving slowly, she tried each of her limbs
in turn and found them all responsive, if a little stiff.
The only hurt she felt was to her ribs, and that was
obviously due to contact with the stump that had stopped her fall.

Fully conversant with the dangers of lying too long
in the cushioning softness of drifted snow, she struggled
to her feet, putting a hand to her ribs when they
tugged with pain at her breathing. The scene was, if
anything, more desolate than ever, but she was some
distance nearer to the belt of trees and the broken
tree stump had probably saved her life.

There was no sign of Claude's footprints nearby, but
she hardly expected there to be this far down. Almost
defeated for a moment, she looked upwards to where the
café stood out like a beacon of warmth and light against

the craggy whiteness of the Maiden's Tower, and the cables of the cableway hung in dark garlands above the ski slopes.

The climb back looked impossible, and yet somehow she had to make it. Rescue work must be concentrated on finding Claude, not on her. Other trees had been broken, probably in some past avalanche, and several dark stumps thrust like broken teeth through the powdery white snow. But one caught her eye that was not merely an upright, but had a curious crosspiece at its base, and after a moment Sophie's pulse began to beat harder and faster as she scrambled her way towards it.

It was only a matter of a few metres, but her ribs hurt so much that she was gasping with pain as she struggled against the slope, scrabbling wildly in the yielding snow with her gloved hands in an effort to help her progress.

Gaining her objective at last, she dropped to her knees beside the ragged stump and reached out to touch what had looked like a crosspiece lying at its base. It was soft and, thank heaven, still warm, and Sophie gathered it into her arms and hugged it close to her, her own predicament forgotten for the moment.

'Claude!'

She pressed her own chilled face to Claude's and closed her eyes for a second in sheer relief. He wasn't fully conscious, but he made a curious whimpering sound and stirred when she held him to the warmth of her body, and she closed her eyes once more to offer up a small prayer.

Looking upwards the ascent seemed impossible, but she wondered if she dared wait for help to arrive, or if Claude had already been too long in the cold. Carrying him presented her with an impossible task. Not only because of the pain in her ribs, she could have borne that somehow, but Claude was a dead weight in her arms and he was a big child for nearly five years old. She could not hope to make any kind of progress up that steep incline and through powder snow carrying an unconscious child, and she felt a sudden impatient anger at her own helplessness.

Two of them huddled together were warmer and more conspicuous against the snow, but the distance was such and the moonlight so deceptive that they probably looked like nothing more than just another broken tree. Speed in finding them was essential for Claude's sake and yet she felt so bruised and so maddeningly helpless that all she could do for the moment was to squat back against the stump of a dead tree.

It was quiet; a shiveringly brittle quiet, emphasised by the chilling softness of the wind, until she looked up suddenly when another, different and more distant sound reached her. From the plateau of rock where the café stood she could have sworn she caught the sound of voices, for just a second, and with her head lifted she listened, her eyes searching the slopes while she held her breath.

Instinctively drawing Claude closer to her in her anxiety to be right, she felt something pressing against her hipbone, something hard and round that jogged her memory and brought a glimmer of hope, however small. The movement cost her dearly, and her forehead was damp with perspiration, but with Claude cradled on her lap she managed to reach round into the pocket of her trousers and take out her compact.

Her father had bought it for her last birthday and it was one of those with a tiny light set in the lid that illuminated the mirror. It was not much, but it was something to encourage her from her present frustrating sense of helplessness, and she grasped any fragment of encouragement eagerly. Her fingers were clumsy in thick gloves, and they trembled anxiously as she coped practically one-handed, but eventually she had the lid open and looked down at her own face reflected eerily against the purple darkness of the night sky.

Shutting it off for a moment, she looked down at Claude, his face pale and small against her breast. He was either asleep from exhaustion or unconscious, and she dared not speculate on which it was at the moment, but hugged him closer as she listened, almost holding her breath, for another sound. She could hear nothing with sufficient clarity to identify it, for the mountains played as many tricks with sound as with sight, and especially at night, but she went on listening and watching.

The windows of the café appeared as no more than a slash of brilliance that seemed incredibly distant, but she told herself that she did not imagine the brief appearance of dark silhouettes that fluttered across it, then disappeared again, like moths against a candle flame, and she closed her fingers tightly around the compact in her hand. Opening the lid once more, she directed the minute glimmer of light towards the summit.

It seemed such a very long time before anything happened, and the light in the compact began to flicker and weaken after what seemed such a short time. The battery that powered it would be very small, she realised with dismay, and not meant for prolonged use. She had to conserve its energy until some more definite sign of rescue appeared, so reluctantly she closed it down and once more held Claude in both arms, bending over to envelop him in her own sparse warmth.

She must have drifted into a half-sleep, and when she opened her eyes it took her a moment or two to identify the lights that moved at the top of the slope. She felt curiously drowsy and incredibly tired physically and it was difficult to concentrate, but then she realised that the voices she had heard were nearer now, and more easily identifiable as human voices. And whoever it was carried torches.

Small beams danced and fluttered over the snow in sweeping half circles, searching for footprints in the way that she had followed Claude's. The moonlight was too thin for her to see much more once they began to descend, but she opened the lid of the compact again and propped it on the tree stump above her head, then sat huddled with Claude in her arms, trying to concentrate on the flickering torches as they came, so very slowly it seemed, down the slope.

Once she thought they were very close and she raised an arm to signal, forgetting the hurt to her ribs, and a great thud of pain took her breath away and made her head spin for a moment. She must have cried out too, for the torchlights were stilled for a second and, in the brittle stillness, she could almost sense people listening.

Then the fluttering beams began their descent once more, taking a slightly different course, so that Sophie knew she had been spotted. Closing her eyes, she leaned her aching body over the small, still figure in her arms. It would not be too long now.

'Sophie! Sophie!'

She was on her feet, Sophie realised dazedly, and held firmly against the warm softness of a ski-jacket, But beneath the jacket was the taut, familiar strength of

Karl's body, and he almost shuddered with the urgency of his relief as he bound her close with a steely arm that threatened to crush her already painful ribs, and slapped lightly but firmly at her cheek.

'Open your eyes, Sophie! Come, *Liebling*, open your eyes!'

She missed the bulk of Claude in her arms, and Karl's insistent voice roused her from an incredible drowsiness that was hard to throw off at first. 'No, Karl—don't do that!' She was hurt enough, and he was adding to her hurt by holding her so tightly that she turned her head from side to side in protest.

'Come, *Liebling*, you must wake up! You are not hurt and you *must* wake up! Sophie—open your eyes!'

She did not remember slipping into semi-consciousness, but she supposed she must have done, and Karl was doing his best to bring her out of it; he could not know how her ribs hurt. Looking up into the tanned face that hovered over her, she noticed how much darker and stronger it looked, and somehow older in the shadowy moonlight—and quite suddenly very relieved when she opened her eyes.

'Sophie!' The hand that had brought her back to wakefulness was curved about her cheek, its strong fingers stroking her cold face, and despite the words he spoke, his voice held no trace of anger, only a gentle scolding. 'I should be angry with you for doing this; I should—Oh, what can I do with you?'

The crushing arm about her body hurt her bruises, but she did not want to lose the touch of him yet, so she bore it for a while. 'I—I couldn't get back up the slope, I——'

'Of course you could not climb any further with Claude in your arms; we know that, *Liebling*, but it is very fortunate that you are not hurt. To try to climb such a slope carrying a child!' A brief jerk of his head indicated the signs of her desperate struggle to reach Claude, and she did not trouble to correct his impression yet, but suddenly remembered that she did not yet know about Claude.

'Claude!' She looked up at him anxiously. 'Is Claude all right?'

'Anton and Robert St John have taken him and he will soon be in hospital, but you, little one, you allowed yourself to fall asleep, and you should know how dangerous that can be in these conditions.'

'I saw your lights coming, and I thought we were going to be all right—I didn't intend to fall asleep.'

She was reproachful, resigned to being considered foolish and impulsive, and she wished she had more inclination to challenge his opinion. Instead, when his arm tightened about her and made her gasp in pain, she buried her face against him and closed her eyes.

'Sophie! You are hurt!'

The voice against her ear was harsh with anxiety and his sudden concern was somehow very satisfying, so that she actually managed a smile when she looked up at him again. He eased his hold without actually releasing her altogether, watching her face in the moonlight.

'It's my ribs.' An attempted laugh made her wince painfully. 'I rolled down the slope and brought up against a tree stump; I've bruised my ribs.'

'Oh, *Liebling*, and I have been holding you so tightly!'

'I didn't mind.'

She made the admission without hesitation, and after a second Karl bent down and pressed his lips briefly and warmly to her cheek. 'You should have told me that you were hurt, little one. I must get you to the top as quickly as I can. Can you manage with me to help, or are you badly enough hurt to need the stretcher?' He glanced upwards to where other figures moved about on the edge of the plateau. 'The rescue team are here now, and they could take you in comfort.'

'Oh no, no!' Relinquishing that strong arm in favour of the rescue sled did not strike Sophie as an exchange for the better, and she clung to Karl with both hands. 'I can make it to the top, if you can cope with me.'

His laughter was unexpected, vibrating against her bruised ribs as he bent his head once more and kissed her mouth. 'I can cope with you, little one! Now—hold tightly to me, *hein*?'

Her mouth set firmly against the throbbing hurt in her side, Sophie nodded. 'I mean to!' she told him.

Sophie would like to have seen Claude, to assure herself of his chance of recovery, but by the time she and Karl reached the Maiden's Tower, he was already on his way down in the cable-car and on his way to hospital.

The last stage of her own climb had been completed with the assistance of the mountain rescue team, and Karl had insisted that she submit to a thorough examination, although she had insisted that her injuries were no worse than bruised ribs. It would have taken little, she thought, for him to order an overnight stay in hospital to be sure.

She appreciated his concern. After her months with Flora it was gratifying to have someone worrying about her, but the authoritative way in which he treated her was discomfitingly reminiscent of her father. She disliked his being so paternal, and said as much to him after he had helped her from the car and left Anton to garage it while he saw her into the house.

'You dislike me taking care of you?'

He sounded more amused than surprised, and a quick glance confirmed the suspicion, so that she frowned. 'I didn't say that, Karl—I just don't like you sounding quite so much like a father figure. I told you once before, I wish you wouldn't treat me as you do the boys.'

Karl opened the front door and ushered her inside with a hand carefully placed in the small of her back and well clear of the bruised ribs, and she caught a provocative gleam in his eyes as the warmth and brightness of the hall enveloped them. He stripped off his own coat and gloves as he stepped through the door after her, and he turned to help her unfasten her jacket, divesting her of it and the thick gloves she wore, just as he might have done for Hans or Hugo.

With her jacket draped over his arm he gave her a broad grin that crinkled the tanned skin at the corners of his eyes and showed his white teeth in contrast to the darkness of his face. 'I do not recall ever kissing one of the boys in quite the same way that I once kissed you, *Liebling*!'

He did not wait for reactions, but walked over and put away her things in the clothes cupboard, leaving Sophie staring after him until she hastily pulled herself together and tugged off her hat. Lisa came out from the sitting-room when she heard them, and glanced swiftly from one to the other, unable to determine the reason for Sophie's obvious discomfiture.

'Ah, you are safely back—good!' The door was still open and she looked across at it. 'Anton is putting away the car?'

'He is!' Karl laughed as he came back, and bent to kiss her cheek, obviously in a high good humour. 'Do not worry, Lisa, I have brought him safely back to you!'

'Oh, but of course you have.' His manner puzzled her, and she did not question it at the moment, but remembered the reason they had all gone out. 'Has the little boy been found? He's safe?'

She asked the question of Sophie, who nodded. 'He's safe, Lisa, but he's in hospital. He was in a pretty bad way when he was found.'

'Little Claude.' Pity showed in Lisa's gentle blue eyes. 'Is he hurt?'

It was Karl who answered, before Sophie could re-assure her, and in such a way that Sophie stared at him for a second or two in stunned surprise. 'He had taken the cable-car to the café by Mädchen Turm and walked out into the snow. He owes his life to Sophie, for if she had not remembered how much he loved to ride the cable to the top he might not have been found until it was much too late.'

The tribute was so completely unexpected that it took Sophie's breath away, but at the same time brought a glowing warmth to her whole body that showed itself in a bright flush that spread gradually over her cheeks as she shook her head. If they had not been found when they had, both she and Claude might not have survived, but he made no condemnation of her rash and impulsive attempt at a lone rescue, and she wondered how he resisted it.

'I just happened to know him very well, Karl. That's why I wanted to come with you. But if you and Anton and Robert hadn't found us——' She shivered, winc-

ing when the movement reminded her that she had not
come off quite scot free.

'Oh, but how fortunate you remembered, Sophie!'
Lisa was obviously putting herself in Flora's shoes, and
imagining how she would feel if it had been Hugo or
Hans in similar circumstances. 'Your cousin must be
so grateful to you.'

It had not even crossed Sophie's mind until now to
wonder just what Flora's reaction had been. Maybe
Karl had seen her at the hospital while Sophie was with
the doctor—he hadn't said. She had not set eyes on her
herself, so she had no idea whether or not Flora was
grateful—but she thought it was unlikely.

A glance at Karl gave no indication at all, but Anton,
who had come in and heard what Lisa said, took off his
coat, making some comment in his own tongue, turning
back to Sophie with a rueful grin. 'I am sorry, Sophie. I
know that she is your cousin, but she is an ungrateful
and completely selfish woman, and I am glad that Karl
has seen her true worth at last!'

Sophie remembered Karl's aggressive and contemptu-
ous attitude towards Flora at the hotel, and wondered
why he did not immediately confirm what Anton said.
Instead he took Sophie's hat from her and placed it
with studied care on a small table beside him.

'Flora is a selfish and very silly woman,' he said, in a
voice that suggested no reproach to his brother for his
opinion, but merely stated a fact. 'She is also lonely
and rather unsure of herself, and I am not particularly
proud of the way I spoke to her tonight.'

'But you were right, Karl!'

Anton did not understand his attitude, and to Sophie
it was completely inexplicable, but she watched him

from below half-closed lids, trying to accept that he had
reacted as he had purely from concern for Claude. She
had recognised at the time that he had been almost
brutally harsh with Flora, but she did not understand
her present feeling of resentment that he now sought to
make excuses for her.

Lisa, perhaps sensing some underlying cause that she
did not know about, took her husband's arm and
headed him in the direction of the sitting-room. 'Let us
all go in here and you can tell me all about it, eh?'

'You and Anton go, Lisa, I will follow in a moment.'

Sophie felt so tired she would have liked to go to bed
and sleep, but she was unprepared for Karl to take a
hand the way he did. She would have complied with
Lisa's invitation, but Karl was shaking his head and he
had a hand on each shoulder with his fingers pressing
firmly into her flesh as he held her there.

'Sophie has some very painful bruises, and she is so
sleepy she can barely keep her eyes open. It is better
that she goes straight to bed, eh, little one?'

Inevitably, of course, Lisa looked concerned and
came back to her, looking into her face anxiously.
'Sophie, I did not know that you are hurt! I am so
sorry.'

'Oh, it isn't anything serious, Lisa, really.' A frown
conveyed her dislike of Karl's haste to pack her off to
bed. 'I'm just a bit bruised, that's all. I fell and hurt my
ribs on a tree stump and they ache a bit, nothing worse.'

'And you have been advised to rest.' Karl would not
be denied, and his eyes as well as the firm set of his
mouth challenged her to deny it. 'It is very late and I
promised the doctor that I would see to it that you took
the sedative he gave you and went immediately to bed.'

'The doctor?'

Lisa frowned anxiously, and Sophie once more blamed Karl with a brief, reproachful look. 'It's just my ribs, that's all.'

'By good fortune, that is all!' Karl interposed swiftly. He was apparently bent on making the most of the incident, and Sophie wished she understood him. 'Not only did this foolish girl set off alone to look for Claude on the mountainside, but after she had fallen and hurt herself, she fell asleep in the snow.'

'Oh, Karl, stop making mountains out of molehills!'

She was aware of Lisa's mounting interest, and Karl seemed determined to relate the whole incident as if she had done everything wrong. After his earlier tribute to her help in finding Claude, she found it hard to understand him. His eyes gleamed like blue gems between their thick lashes, and she would have sworn he was enjoying the whole thing, except that his mouth looked so firm and tight.

'You could have died, *Liebling*—you and Claude both, and I do not find it easy to accept the fact of how close you came to dying out there!'

That frequently used endearment was Sophie's undoing; she shook her head and, instead of making indignant denials as she meant to, she spoke mildly and in a small voice that showed just how tired she really was.

'You found us,' she said, and Karl nodded, putting his hands on her upper arms and bringing that irresistibly forceful personality to bear.

'We found you, Sophie, but we might not have done, and I do not want my effort to have been for nothing. So—will you not go to bed and sleep?'

'I suppose so.' It was so much easier to comply, she found, though she once again experienced that same prickling resentment at the tone of his voice.

'But of course you must rest and sleep.' She heard Lisa's murmur of approval and thought she had turned away. 'Goodnight, Sophie, sleep well.'

Sophie could not see past him, but she was aware of Lisa and Anton going on into the sitting-room and the door closing behind them, leaving her in the hall with Karl. They turned and walked in the direction of the stairs, with Karl's hand on her shoulder, as if to be sure she did not change her mind, and stopped at the foot of the stairs.

Without raising her eyes too high, she could watch the sensual mobility of Karl's mouth, and notice that it was half-smiling, almost as if he anticipated her protest.

'I don't like being sent to bed, Karl.'

'Like one of the boys?'

He laughed and gently pulled her into his arms, folding her as close as he could and still make sure he did not hurt her too much. Then he found her mouth and pressed his own firmly over its softness, a kiss that was deep and searching and seemed to touch every nerve in her body.

It was like being borne along on some irresistible tide that she made no attempt to oppose, and even the ache in her ribs was drowned in the wild excitement of being kissed as she had never been kissed before. He released her slowly and looked down into her face, smiling and soft-voiced.

'Does that make you feel a little less like one of the boys?' he asked, and brushed her lips with the tempting warmth of his mouth. 'Goodnight, little one—sleep well!'

CHAPTER NINE

It was still hard for Sophie to believe she was where she was, or that she was dancing with Karl, but there was nothing ethereal about the lean sensuousness of the body that moved in unison with hers, or the tanned face that smiled down at her, crinkling the corners of his blue eyes.

It was strange in one way to think of him as a dancing man, for his natural environment always seemed to be the snowy slopes of the ski-runs, and the cold, clean air of the mountains. And yet he seemed quite at home on the crowded dance-floor, and his impeccable sense of rhythm, she supposed had quite a lot to do with his skiing.

Even in the close and slightly over-heated atmosphere of the restaurant, he looked fresh and clear-eyed, his hair thick and gleaming and inevitably falling from its place above his brow into a broad swathe across half his forehead. He smelled of some fresh, masculine scent too that she did not recognise, but assumed it was probably French or Swiss.

The situation was something Sophie had dreamed of often in the old days, which seemed so much longer ago than three years. But then he had not moved in the same social circle as her and her father. During the day, or on the terrace of their hotel, he and her father would often talk together and became quite good

friends for the duration of their stay, but his evening
activities had never included starry-eyed eighteen-year-
old girls who worshipped him from afar.

For a week after her single-handed attempt to rescue
Claude, she had seen very little of Karl. Not that she
was too surprised, for he had to practise hard if he was
to do as well as he hoped in the coming championships,
but she was rather disturbed to realise how much she
missed him. The thing that stayed persistently and discomfitingly in her mind, however, was whether or not
he had also been seeing Flora.

After his expression of sympathy for Flora, when he
spoke to Anton after they came back from Brunnenheim, it seemed more than likely that he would offer
her his sympathy while Claude was in hospital. And
that was a situation that Sophie found particularly unacceptable.

Then yesterday he had come to Schläfing to visit
Lisa and his new niece, and quite out of the blue, informed Sophie that she was having dinner with him in
Brunnenheim. It took her so by surprise that at first she
did nothing but stare at him, and Karl had laughed and
lifted her chin on one big hand while he looked down
into her face, asking if she did not approve of dining
and dancing after a day's work.

Whether the idea of bringing her to the Schillenberg
Hotel had any significance, she had no way of telling,
but Karl had watched her face while he told her their
destination and laughed when she looked surprised.
Now she was dancing in Karl's arms around a room
where she had all too often watched Flora enjoying herself, and not been allowed to join in.

A long and ornately embroidered skirt and a silky
sweater made her slim figure look taller than it actually

was, although when she was close to Karl the illusion
was lost, for he was almost head and shoulders taller
than she was. It had seemed strange too, to sit down to
a meal in the Schillenbergs' restaurant without Claude,
but she had enjoyed this dinner more than she remembered enjoying anything before. In fact the whole evening so far had seemed more like part of a dream than an
actual happening, and she felt dreamy as well as quite
incredibly happy as she danced.

Karl was smiling at her, she realised suddenly, and
shook off her dreaminess as she smiled. 'It is your turn
to take the floor, eh, little one? Instead of standing at
the edge of the crowd as you used to, looking like a
lovely, lost little creature who dare not show her face.'

She did not like to think he had seen her as some
kind of ill-used little underling constantly at Flora's
beck and call, and yet she supposed it had been true, although she had tried to close her eyes to it. Conscious of
the hand that held her close and the strong arm enclos-
ing her, she found it hard to go back to the days when
Flora had held such sway over her, even though it was
so recent.

'Did I really look so—so pitiful?'

'Sometimes, *Liebling*!' His eyes had a warm bright
gleam that did quite incredible things to her senses, and
they held her uncertain gaze determinedly. 'Sometimes
I wanted to come and draw you out, make you join in.'

'But you didn't.'

'No.' She looked up at him again curiously, and he
laughed. 'You were so afraid of Flora that I dared not,
Liebling. How could I make things even more difficult
for you, eh?'

It was not a welcome reminder, and she tried hard
not to believe that the only reason she was here now was

because he felt sorry for her, and wanted to make up
something of what she had missed when she was with
Flora. She could not bear the thought of this evening
being prompted simply by pity, and there was a certain
note in her voice when she challenged him with it that
he could not miss.

'So you felt sorry for me!'

'No.' The short and frankly honest answer was not
what she expected and she blinked uncertainly for a
moment. Shaking his head, Karl laughed at her. 'I was
sometimes impatient with you, little one, for allowing
yourself to be—put upon?—the way you did. I wanted
to shake you and make you show some of the spirit I remembered you had when you were eighteen!'

Something caught her breath when she looked up at
him. 'You remember what I was like at eighteen? It was
three years ago!'

'Of course I remember—I never forget a pretty
woman, especially when she hides on the slopes to
watch me practise!'

'Oh, Karl!' She was blushing and there was nothing
she could do about it. His reminding her of her youthful and, as she had always believed, secret admiration of
him, startled her and she wondered how often he had
laughed at her starry-eyed adoration in the old days. 'I
didn't realise.' She glanced up at him, a hint of reproach on her mouth. 'I suppose you found it very
funny.'

'On the contrary,' he denied, smiling down at her, 'I
was very flattered and in fact I confess, I even showed
off for you sometimes.'

It was a confession she would never have expected of
him, and it somehow made him so human that she
seemed to come closer to him than ever before. 'I don't

believe it!' She shook her head, but in her heart she believed it, because she wanted to believe it. It mattered to her what Karl thought and did, she realised, more than ever it had three years ago; and the realisation made her feel suddenly light-headed.

'You think I would lie to you?'

It seemed to Sophie suddenly that nothing could go wrong with this wonderful evening, and she was laughing, her eyes bright and clear as amber, with that intriguing tilt at their corners. 'I know you wouldn't lie to me,' she told him, her mouth softly teasing as she looked up at him. 'You believe in being blunt, you've shown that once this evening when you told me what a—a mouse I was when I was with Flora!'

The arm about her tightened slightly, reminding her of the not quite healed bruises on her ribs, and Karl bent his head until his mouth brushed the soft skin beside her ear, a low soft flutter of laughter tickling her neck. 'You are still a little mouse, *Liebling*!'

'Karl!'

For all his teasing her, there was something in the way he held her and the gleaming blueness of his eyes that brought a reaction from her senses that she could do nothing to control. Dancing in his arms it was all too easy to feel as she had three years ago, and that was something she had vowed not to let happen this time.

An arm encircled her waist still, but she was turned around suddenly and headed towards the huge archway that led from the restaurant into the reception hall of the hotel, weaving and ducking between the couples on the dance-floor, and she looked up at him enquiringly but offered no resistance. It was enough that he still had that strong arm about her.

He smiled briefly and mysteriously when he went to

fetch their top coats and helped her into hers still
without enlightening her, so that she felt bound, eventually, to question him. 'Where are we going, Karl?
Where are you taking me?'

When he smiled she could feel her limbs tremble,
there was something in his eyes that seemed to reach
her very soul and make her feel she was walking above
the ground. With both hands she turned up the collar
of her coat, framing her small flushed face with the softness of dark fur, and Karl's smile quizzed her.

'Will you come with me wherever I take you, little
one?' he asked, and she nodded, without even pausing
to consider.

Taking her hand, he laughed, squeezing her fingers
hard, then tucking her arm under his as he led her
across the reception hall. They were still some distance
from the outside doors when someone called out from
behind them, and Karl turned swiftly.

'Karl, *mon chéri*!'

The voice was familiar to Sophie too, and she turned
a second after Karl did, and gazed at the Comtesse Dauzan. A tall elegant woman in her fifties, she was just as
Sophie remembered her from her early days with Flora
in Paris. Paris clothes and a slim, almost bony figure
betrayed the Comtesse's former profession as surely as
the same type of figure did Flora's, and she had an
incredibly youthful face still.

'Louise!'

It was startling to find Karl so familiar with her, but
then both were widely travelled, and the Comtesse was
an attractive woman, no matter what her years. He took
her hand and raised it to his lips in a gesture that for
some reason rather surprised Sophie, then he murmured something in French which the Comtesse

seemed to appreciate, judging by her smile.

Turning to Sophie, Karl drew her forward with that strong and reassuring arm about her waist again. 'You know Sophie Roberts, do you not, Louise?'

'Indeed I do. *Mademoiselle.*' The Comtesse's shrewd but kindly eyes had a speculative look as they scanned Sophie from head to toe, and she raised a slim dark brow. 'You look more happy than when I saw you last, child. Is Flora treating you with more consideration, perhaps?'

'I'm not with Flora any longer, Comtesse.'

That elegant brow once more questioned the situation and this time it was clear she expected Karl to enlighten her. 'I had heard so, but I found it hard to believe that anyone could leave a child who was so devoted to her. Perhaps if this had not been so, this dreadful—accident might not have occurred.'

Whether or not Karl was prepared to explain her position, Sophie preferred to make her own explanations, and she looked at the Comtesse with an unmistakable gleam of challenge in her eyes and her chin angled in a way there was no denying.

'I did not leave Claude, Comtesse, Flora gave me no option. She dismissed me!'

'So!' Shrewd dark eyes fell unerringly on Karl. 'And you will no doubt be fully aware of the reason for such a foolish gesture, will you not, *mon brave?*'

There was little doubt why Louise Dauzan was in Brunnenheim. Someone, and it was unlikely to have been Flora, had told her not only of Claude's situation, but that Sophie was no longer in charge of him too. She was there to see for herself and, knowing the Comtesse's temper and her devotion to her grandson, Sophie could almost feel sorry for Flora.

But the hotel lobby was not the place for such matters to be discussed, Sophie felt, although neither Karl nor the Comtesse seemed to be concerned about the fact that there were people constantly to and fro. Seeing her evening brought to an abrupt end if the Comtesse insisted on pursuing the matter with Karl, Sophie felt a churning resentment to realise that even now Flora's affairs could intrude on her private life.

'You are here to see Claude?' Karl neatly side-stepped the question of his being responsible for Sophie's dismissal, and the Comtesse nodded.

'I am here to take him home to France,' she said firmly. 'His father is concerned that he is being so neglected, and he will not allow such a situation to continue.'

'You're—you're taking him away from Flora?'

She had little sympathy for Flora, heaven knew, but Sophie dared not speculate how angry she would be if Claude was taken out of her charge. She was a selfish and greedy woman and she saw her son mainly as an insurance, an access to the Dauzan fortune when he eventually inherited from his father. She would not easily relinquish such an advantage.

The Comtesse had few illusions about her daughter-in-law, she knew her too well, and she was looking at Sophie as if she suspected her sympathy was misplaced. 'You think that unduly harsh, Miss Roberts?'

'Oh, no!' Sophie could not claim to think Claude would be better off with Flora than with his grandmother, no matter how harsh the basic fact was. 'It's the best thing for Claude, and I'm glad he's going back with you for his sake.'

'Sensible child!' The shrewd eyes regarded her

steadily for a moment. 'You would not consider returning to France with me? I seem to recall that Claude was
very fond of you.'

'Oh no, Comtesse, I can't, I'm sorry.'

She had felt the beginnings of a similar reply in
Karl and hastily forestalled him, but even so he followed up her refusal with an explanation, as if he
wanted there to be no doubt about it. 'Sophie is caring
for my brother's children at the moment, Louise. Lisa
has recently had another baby and Sophie is helping.'

'Ah!' The explanation seemed to satisfy her, and she
was giving her attention to Karl once more. There was
a humourless smile about her bright red mouth and a
glitter in her eyes at the prospect before her. 'Flora
will not easily accept the position, I suspect. Karl,
perhaps you—You have such charm, *mon chéri*, and if
there was a broad shoulder on which to weep, *hein*?'

'My dear Louise, I am sorry! I cannot do that even
to please an old friend; I am sure you understand.'

He was so firm about it that Sophie looked at him in
surprise, though oddly enough the Comtesse seemed to
accept his reaction much more readily. She merely
shrugged her shoulders and glanced at Sophie in a way
that left her meaning in no doubt.

'Ah, but of course! In that case, *mon chéri*, I will
leave you to your own affairs!'

Taking her hand once more, Karl kissed her fingers
as he had when they met, offering no further explanation of his adamant refusal to become involved with
Flora. 'I am sorry, Louise, that I cannot help you.'

'Ah, *mais non*!' His apology was dismissed with an
airy hand and there was a look on the Comtesse's lean
autocratic face that promised ill for any objection
Flora might produce. 'It is not your concern, *mon cher*

Karl; I am only thankful that you have not been foolish enough to become Flora's second husband. It is not a role I would wish upon any man for whom I had the slightest regard. I have seen what it has done to my son.'

'It will not be easy—what you have to do.'

It looked almost as if he might be having second thoughts about becoming involved, and Sophie found herself praying that he would not. But the Comtesse looked well able to deal with any opposition, she thought, and saw her guess confirmed when a gloved forefinger tapped the outside of her handbag.

'I have an order here that allows me to return Claude to his father. I shall fetch him from the hospital tomorrow, and the matter will be ended! It will not be easy, *mon chéri*, but I will deal with it, have no fear!'

The lobby was for the most part quiet at the moment, only one or two people passing through it, but it was possible to catch the faint whirring sound of the lift descending before the doors opened and released more people from its confines to spread in different directions.

'Karl!'

Neither he nor the Comtesse seemed to have noticed that among the newcomers were Flora and Robert St John, but her softly spoken warning and a hand on his arm drew Karl's immediate attention to them. He said nothing, but squeezed her fingers, and she noticed a certain icy speculation in his blue eyes as he watched Flora's progress across the lobby, walking just a fraction of a step ahead of Robert.

She glittered, Sophie thought a little dazedly. Tall and thin as a boy in velvet and fur, her yellow-blonde head bare as it so often was, and Sophie's heart was in her mouth when Flora caught sight of them and hesitated a second before changing direction. Automatically Robert followed suit, though he looked plainly discomfited, and Sophie felt a brief moment of impatience for his blind devotion to her cousin.

Flora had a brittle, glossy brightness that was as artificial as the kind of life she led, and Sophie wished she better understood the sympathy she felt for her. Flora could have no idea what was in store for her, or she would have avoided a public confrontation with her erstwhile mother-in-law.

Clinging tightly to Robert's arm, she looked at the Comtesse with an ill-concealed air of defiance, completely ignoring Karl and Sophie for the moment. She spoke in the high-pitched and sharp voice that Sophie had learned to recognise as not simply bad-tempered, but anxious and defiant too.

'I didn't know you were expected, Maman! Are you here to see Claude?'

'I am here to take him home to his father.' The Comtesse had never believed in beating about the bush, and Sophie heard the sharp hiss of Flora's indrawn breath.

She said nothing for a moment, then she turned like a cat on Sophie, the words coming through clenched teeth. 'You did this! You sent for her; you meant to get back at me one way or the other, didn't you?'

'No, Flora!'

Karl had said she was a little mouse, but at the moment Sophie had never felt less mouselike and inoffensive. She was angry, and the curious fact was that she was angry in part because she could still feel sorry for Flora, even after all she had said and done. She controlled her voice with an effort, keeping to a level that she hoped would not attract attention.

'I didn't even tell the Comtesse that Claude was in hospital, Flora, though perhaps I should have done, for his sake!'

Strangely enough in the circumstances, Sophie thought she was believed, but for the moment Flora simply stood clutching tightly to Robert's arm and saying nothing. She did not like the alternative, that was clear, and she hesitated to accuse Karl. But she had to know, however much she would dislike the answer, and she turned on him at last, her eyes narrowed and cold as ice.

'You——'

'It was Bernhard Grüber who wrote to me, Flora, not Sophie or Karl!' Louise Dauzan's clear voice cut across the accusation, and Flora stared at her.

'The proprietor of this hotel?'

The Comtesse nodded. 'I have been a valued client here for many years, and Bernhard did not wish to lose my patronage. You had, I believe, left my grandson in the care of hotel servants when he ran off. It was because he feared my reaction to such a fact that I was informed. You were in the habit of doing so, I understand.'

Flora looked stunned, it showed in her face, though she probably did not realise quite how starkly it showed. There was a dead, flat look about her, bereft of her customary self-confident sparkle, and she did not know what to do but cling as tightly as possible to Robert.

'But—you can't just walk in and—and take him.'

Once more that sharp forefinger tapped her handbag, and the Comtesse's lean, proud features showed a hint of cruelty as she played her last trump card. 'Ah, but indeed I can. I have an order here authorising me to do so!'

'He's my son!'

'He is also Rudi Dauzan's heir, which I think is your main interest in him, Flora! If you had sometimes treated the child with the natural love of a mother this would not have been necessary. You have lost your access to the Dauzan millions through your own neglect, *ma fille*! You have no one else to blame!'

Flora looked around her, her face working with the tangled emotions that churned inside her and gave her eyes a sharp, glittering shine that nevertheless recognised defeat. The only face that showed any sign of sympathy was Robert's, and he saw only the hurt he thought she must be feeling. He guessed nothing of the anger and frustration that made her fingers dig so tightly into his flesh, and he covered her hand with his.

'Darling——'

So many times Sophie had seen Flora snatch away her hand at moments like that, but this time she did not. When he squeezed her fingers encouragingly, she allowed him to, and before long the glitter and sparkle began to return, and she smiled. Tossing back her yellow-gold head, she curled her lip, and shrugged carelessly.

'Oh well, that solves a problem!' she said. 'Now I can marry Bobby without having to bother about a child always being around!'

It was so incredibly quiet and peaceful in the cable-car as it swung out over the snowy valley and climbed slowly towards the Maiden's Tower. There was no one else in the car, and Sophie stood with Karl looking down at the deserted slopes that tomorrow would once more be alive with swift, flying figures skimming down towards the village.

Sophie was still too full of the evening's events to give her mind as completely as she would have liked to the present situation. Karl stood immediately behind her, his hand at her waist, and she was comfortably aware of his body half supporting her, and the warmth and strength that emanated from him.

The line of pine trees came into sight below them, scrawled darkly across the white face of the mountain, and she was reminded of that night, a little over a week ago, when she had waited with Claude in her arms for someone to come and find them. Somehow she had been so sure that it would be Karl who came.

The sigh she gave was unconscious and when she turned her head her cheek brushed against Karl's jacket and the broad comfort of his chest. Laying her face on the softness of suede, she half-closed her eyes in a sudden need to ease from the urgent tangle of emotions that had possessed them all down there in the hotel. Up here it was quiet and still and she could relax.

A slight movement brought Karl's head down close to hers and his lips pressed lightly to the lobe of her ear, a long finger brushing the dark hair from her neck with caressing lightness. 'You are still thinking of Flora?'

It had always surprised her to some degree that he could so easily follow her train of thought, and she smiled faintly as she nodded. 'I can't get over her saying she'll marry Robert.' Remembering Flora's cruel assessment of his devotion, she shook her head. 'Poor Robert!'

A tanned cheek rested on the dark softness of her

hair, and his voice fluttered warmly against her ear, threaded with a hint of laughter, she thought. 'He loves her, little one, he will not think himself poor!'

'I suppose not.'

He put an arm around her and pulled her back against him, and she could feel the muscular strength in the arm and the lean hard body that trapped her between them, drawing her closer still until she felt her heart beating with the wild excitement of his nearness. And he pressed his face to hers when she leaned back her head.

'You are not unhappy, are you, *Liebling*?'

'No, of course I'm not!' She laughed, very unsteadily, and put her own two hands over the one that spanned her slimness and must surely feel the thudding beat of her heart under those strong hard fingers. 'I suppose you could say it's a happy ending—for Claude at least, and maybe for Flora too.'

'And for you?'

Unsure how far to commit herself as yet, she laughed and shook her head. 'For me too in a way, although——'

'Although?' His lips brushed the corner of her mouth, a light, searching kiss that made her breathless with its promise. 'You need something more to make your happy ending, eh, *mein Liebling*?'

Sophie dared not answer, there was so much to lose if she broke this enchanted moment, and she simply leaned back against him and looked out at the purple-dark sky and the shimmeringly white peaks in the distance. His hands slid around her, turning her until she faced him, eyes raised just high enough to see the firm sensuality of his mouth.

'Sophie—little one!' A long finger brushed back a

wisp of hair from her forehead, and she saw his mouth curve into a smile. 'Do you know how close I came to falling in love with you once before?' He did not wait for her reply, but went on in a voice so vibrant with urgency that it shivered through her body like fire and ice and made her tremble. 'You were a very lovely child then, *Liebling*, and if you had stayed longer I would have fallen in love with you, no matter if you were so young.'

Sophie thought of the times she had dreamed of that happening. Of being in Karl's arms and hearing his voice telling her how he loved her. Everything she had felt for him then, she felt now, only a thousand times more deeply. The violence of her own emotions startled her so much that she felt almost dizzy with it.

'And now?'

The prompt was breathless and barely above a whisper, and Karl's arms enfolded her so closely to him that she could feel every muscle striving to draw her even closer. He bent his head and touched her mouth with his, lightly and gently.

'And now, *Liebling*, you are a woman. You are still so young, but you are a woman with the feelings of a woman, and I love you more than I ever dreamed I could love anyone!'

'Oh, Karl!' Flora no longer had even a fraction of her thoughts; there was no one but her and Karl in this small, dim-lit world suspended above the snowy valley, and she clung to him tightly, almost fearful, even now, that her dream would end again. 'I thought I loved you—when we met that first time. I used to watch you, to want to be with you, just to be where you were. I didn't think it was possible to love you any more than I did then, but I do!'

He had known, she knew that now. From that teasing remark he had made about her watching him on the slopes when she thought herself unseen. He must have guessed how she felt about him, and he had probably been gently amused, even though he claimed now to have been on the brink of falling in love with her.

Leaning back in his arms, she looked up into the strong face with its lean contours shaded and darkened by the dim light, and the blue eyes that crinkled at their corners when he smiled. That sensual mouth that could make her forget everything when he kissed her.

'You must have found me quite an embarrassment,' she said, and begged him with her eyes to deny it, which he did, promptly and without hesitation.

'Never an embarrassment, *Liebling*, you were too lovely to cause me embarrassment, and I *could* have loved you, if there had been time. You left me too soon, and I never thought to see you again.'

His hands held her as if he meant never to let her go again, and when she stirred he bound her close in his arms and sought her mouth with an urgency that kindled her own responses to heights she had never dreamed of.

'You will marry me?' It was not so much a demand as a plea for reassurance, Sophie recognised, and she put her hands to the lean, tanned face and smiled, her fingers stroking gently over the warmth of his mouth. 'Sophie, *mein Liebling*!'

The cable-car was coming to the end of its journey, and soon the doors would slide apart, letting in the cold mountain air, where broad streamers of yellow light from the café windows reached out towards the Maiden's Tower, looming like a fortress against the night sky. Crowned with snow, a monument to a lost love, as she had thought her own to be.

She gave herself up once more to the possession of Karl's mouth and the hard urgency of his arms, then lifted her face and smiled when he allowed her breathing space at last. 'I'll marry you, my love. I've waited so long, how can I refuse?'

Have you missed any of these best-selling Harlequin Romances?

By popular demand... to help complete your collection of Harlequin Romances

48 titles listed on the following pages...

Harlequin Reissues

Harlequin Reissues

Complete and mail this coupon today!

In every issue...

Here's what you'll find:

♥ a complete, full-length romantic novel...illustrated in color.

♥ exotic travel feature...an adventurous visit to a romantic faraway corner of the world.

♥ delightful recipes from around the world...to bring delectable new ideas to your table.

♥ reader's page...your chance to exchange news and views with other Harlequin readers.

♥ other features on a wide variety of interesting subjects.

Start enjoying your own copies of Harlequin magazine immediately by completing the subscription reservation form.

Not sold in stores!